Also by Patrick Irelan

Memoir:

Central Standard: a time, a place, a family
A Firefly in the Night: A Son of the Middle West

Short Stories:

Reruns
The Miracle Boy

The Big Drugstore

Patrick Irelan

Ice Cube Press Est. 1993
North Liberty, Iowa

The Big Drugstore
Copyright © 2015 Patrick Irelan

Isbn 9781888160871

Library of Congress Control Number: 2015931947

Ice Cube Press, LLC (Est. 1993)
205 N. Front Street
North Liberty, Iowa 52317
www.icecubepress.com
steve@icecubepress.com
twitter: @icecubepress

The paper used in this publication meets the minimum requirements of the American National Standard for Information Sciences—Permanence of Paper for Printed Library Materials, ANSI Z39.48-1992.

Manufactured in the United States of America.

To Dan Lechay

"What did it matter where you lay once you were dead? In a dirty sump or in a marble tower on top of a high hill? You were dead, you were sleeping the big sleep."

—Raymond Chandler

Chapter One

Years of experience in the security business have led me to the formulation of Scofield's Law: If you put enough objects in a convenient location, someone will try to steal them. The value of the objects is irrelevant to the truth of this law. People will steal anything they can move.

I was testing this law one fall night at the Morco Drugstore in downtown Davenport, Iowa, when I spotted a young woman with blond hair and quick hands. "What did you put in your purse?" I said. I already knew the answer. I'd seen her do it.

"What?" She spun around, her big blue eyes fixing on me like a scared baby's.

"The toothpaste," I said. "I saw you put it into your purse." She didn't answer for a moment. We stood there in the middle of one of the long aisles, the glare from the fluorescent lamps overhead reflecting off of every box, can, bottle, and tube.

"I forgot what I was doing," she finally said. "I meant to pay for it."

I gave her a tired, skeptical look. "You'll have to do better than that."

"I'm sorry," she said. "I won't do it again. It's just that we need it, and everything costs so much. My mother lost her job, and I don't make enough to pay for everything."

"Let me see some identification," I said. She fished around in her purse, came up with a driver's license, and handed it over. Her name was Kathy Dove. She was twenty-one years old and lived at 528 Raven Street. I looked back at her and memorized her appearance. She was short, blond, and cute; but her most distinctive feature was the soft innocence of her face. The small birthmark on her right cheek added to this effect. If I hadn't seen her take the toothpaste, I wouldn't have thought her capable of it.

"I won't do it again," she said. "Please don't turn me in. My mother would die. I mean it. She would just die." She searched my face for sympathy. She found it.

I handed back her driver's license. "It's the policy of Morco Drugstores to let first-time shoplifters off with a warning," I said. This was nonsense. Morco's actual policy was to prosecute first-time shoplifters as if they were serial killers. My own policy contained more flexibility, largely because I'm softhearted, sentimental, and an easy mark for young people who are trying to help their mothers.

"I'll add your name to our list," I said. More nonsense. We had no list. "Put the toothpaste back on the shelf, and don't do it again. The next time, I'll call the police." She put it back, walked quickly to the door, and disappeared into the September night.

You might think that a forty-one-year-old man would have something more important to do than guard the toothpaste at Morco Drugstores. Maybe most men of that age do, but at the Scofield Detective Agency we take what we can get, and what we can get is often nothing more than a bar of soap or a mousetrap.

After watching Kathy Dove walk out the door, I looked at my watch. It was 8:45, almost closing time. I took one last stroll through the store, down each brightly lit aisle, past hundreds of products. At the front of the room, cashier Tracy Gibbs was ringing up her last few sales of the day. At the drug counter, pharmacist Brian Walker was filling his last prescription.

At 8:55, I headed for the office at the back of the store to compare notes with Jason King, the manager. The office was small and bleak, with steel furniture and file cabinets, stacks of paperwork, and bare white walls. I found King in his swivel chair with his back to the door, probably lighting a cigarette. "Jason," I said, "this is a smoke-free area. Smoking is bad for your health and bad for your employment."

King didn't laugh. He didn't even chuckle. People get sick to death of my little jokes. I walked over and gave him a playful shove. He tipped forward, fell out of the chair, and sprawled on his side. Blood covered his chest. His face was pale and taut. His eyes stared unblinkingly at the big drugstore that never closes.

†

I pulled the cell phone from the pocket of my suit coat and called 911. A Davenport cop arrived in one minute. An ambulance arrived in three. The paramedics examined King and declared him dead. The butcher knife sticking out of his chest probably gave them their first clue.

Detective Lieutenant Anthony Rocco arrived and asked a lot of pointed questions. Rocco was big, tall, and slow moving. His clothes always looked wrinkled, even when newly pressed. Rocco was usually more polite to me than most cops were. He respected me as a fellow detective. He also respected me as a brother-in-law. He was married to my sister Maggie.

"Did you see who did it?" he said.

"No, sorry," I said.

"Where were you right before you found the body?" he said, scratching the dark stubble on his chin.

"Out on the floor." I gestured toward the sales floor.

"Did you see anything suspicious?"

"There was a young woman pinching a tube of toothpaste."

"Toothpaste?" He stared at me.

"Yeah."

"You were worrying about a shoplifter while not twenty-five yards away someone was murdering the manager?"

"Don't rub it in." I adjusted my tie, even though it didn't need it.

"Who was she?" He scratched his chin again.

"Her name's Kathy Dove. She lives at five twenty-eight Raven Street." I described the shoplifter for him.

"What was she wearing?"

"Blue jeans and a T-shirt."

Rocco pointed at the body. "Take a look at the knife," he said. "Ever see it before?"

"I don't know. I've seen a lot like it. It's a Gerhart-Brooks butcher knife. It sells for eighteen dollars. This store loses about one a month to shoplifters." He looked at me as if I were an idiot. I felt like crawling under a boulder until the next glacier moved it.

"You know anyone who might have had reason to kill him?" he said.

"No, although I haven't worked here all that long. He always acted friendly. Everyone seemed to like him." We both looked at the body. "Almost everyone," I said.

Dr. Cook, the county medical examiner, arrived to conduct his preliminary examination. In his tweed jacket and horn-rimmed glasses, he looked as neat as always. The knife caught his eye, too. Rocco went to talk to the only other employees in the store, Brian Walker and Tracy Gibbs. "Stick around," he told me. "I may need your wise counsel."

When Dr. Cook finally completed his examination and walked out of the office, the evidence technicians went to work with their cameras, tweezers, vacuums, and dusting powder. Rocco spoke to the doctor, then walked back over to me.

"Take a look around the office," he said, scratching his cheek this time instead of his chin. "Then do the same thing out on the floor."

I did as he said, scanning the office, then the store. "Okay," I said.

"Do you see anything out of the ordinary?" He gestured vaguely at the area around us, then focused his dark eyes on mine and waited for something useful. He didn't get it.

"Not really," I said.

"Do you see anything that shouldn't be here?"

"No."

"Is anything missing?"

"No, nothing," I said. "Not even a tube of toothpaste."

Chapter Two

The next morning, I arrived at William Morrison's office at ten-thirty sharp for a ten o'clock appointment. Morrison always kept me waiting at least fifteen minutes, so I'd learned how to cope.

Morrison's office stood on the top floor of a five-story brick edifice in downtown Davenport. The rent was cheap. Morrison owned the building. He also owned the Morco Drug Company, a chain of twenty stores in Iowa and Illinois. His success had resulted from two critical factors: hard work and inheritance. He was the only child of James Morrison, who had founded the company in 1958.

Morrison's middle-aged secretary, Barbara Faber, ushered me into the big man's office, walked back out, and closed the door. Just to remind me who was boss, Morrison kept me waiting while he placed a phone call. I sat down. For ten minutes, Morrison argued with a supplier about a large-quantity discount on toilet paper. I used the time to look around the room, which was as dreary as money could make it. A grape-blue carpet. Flaccid leather chairs.

Lifeless paintings of quail, pheasants, and deer. The place needed the delicate touch of a three-alarm fire.

Finally, Morrison hung up. "You were late," he said.

"Sorry," I said. "I was on the phone with J. Edgar Hoover."

If Morrison found this amusing, he didn't show it. His pale face looked as bland as always. He had the appearance of an ideal shopkeeper: neither tall nor short, fat nor thin. Every strand of his brown hair lay neatly in place. His gray suit was crisp, clean, and as remarkable as a bicarbonate of soda.

"I talked to Chief Mittendorf this morning," he said, adopting his good-citizen voice. "This murder is a horrible thing. He said he had every available officer working on the case."

"I'm sure he does."

"I told him he'd have my complete cooperation with the investigation, and I said I was sure you'd feel the same way. Was I right?"

"You were right."

"Take whatever time you need away from your usual assignment to answer any questions the police have, and show them around as much as necessary."

"Be happy to."

"Of course, when the police don't need your assistance, you can get on with the security work we hired you for."

"I'm afraid not."

His head drew back. His gray eyes stared. "What do you mean?" he said.

"The police are just fine," I said, "but I need to conduct my own investigation."

"Whatever for?"

"Last night somebody murdered Jason King while I was retrieving a four-dollar tube of toothpaste. I can't ignore that kind of nerve. It's as if someone did it to insult me. That's just my ego at work, I realize, but there's something else. I owe it to King. I didn't help him when he needed it. The least I can do is find out who killed him."

"I can understand that, but I still think we should leave it to the police. Something like this scares customers away. It's best to just let people forget it. We don't need someone else going around asking questions. The police will do enough of that."

I didn't say anything. I just gave him the sneer I reserve for greedy druggists. He got the point. "I'm not just thinking about my own welfare," he said. "I opened this new store downtown to help revitalize the area. If we fail, other businesses won't even try."

"Uh-huh," I said. I hoped he wouldn't sprout a halo and turn water into wine. On second thought, the wine would be okay.

"Something like this is bad for business, and that's bad for the whole community."

"Now let me tell you what's bad for me," I said. "I'm in the investigation and security business. While I was at work in one of your stores, someone murdered the manager while I was standing twenty-five yards away with a tube of toothpaste in my ear. That's not the kind of performance people look for in a security service. They like to think they're safer when their private cop is around. I have to solve this murder in order to salvage my reputation. I hope you'll keep me on the payroll while I'm doing it, but I'll stay on the case whether you pay me or not." I paused for dramatic effect. "When we get to the bottom of this, we'll also restore customer confidence in Morco." I didn't know customer confidence from petroleum jelly, but it sounded good.

He pondered awhile. "What will this involve?" he said.

"Talking to people, asking questions, snooping around."

"When do you want to start?"

"Right now."

He paused again. "All right. I hope I'm not making a mistake. Be as unobtrusive as possible."

Morrison seemed relieved to see me go. I walked unobtrusively to the northeast corner of Fourth and Brady, where I had the only office still in use in a three-story brick building. My office stood on the second floor, in the corner overlooking the intersection. Directly below me, a Chinese restaurant occupied the only retail slot still in use at that address. If anyone needed space, there was no waiting list at Fourth and Brady.

I climbed the stairs, unlocked my one-room office, and opened a window to air the place out. The office contained a file cabinet, a coat rack, three chairs, and a desk—all made of oak and all quite old. The room also displayed, to the rare visitor, a radio, a telephone, a small refrigerator, and two windows. One window overlooked Fourth Street. The other overlooked Brady. Two black-and-white photographs hung on the walls. One showed a gravel road passing through Iowa's rolling hills. The other showed the Centennial Bridge, which crosses the Mississippi between Davenport and Rock Island.

I sat down at the desk, picked up the phone, and dialed. "East Moline Morco Drug," a female voice said.

"Let me talk to Sherlock Junior," I said.

The woman giggled. "Hold on, Mike," she said. They know and love me at all twenty Morco Drugstores. I've defended the toothpaste in every one of them.

Time passed. I looked out the window at the blue sky. "Hello, Mike," Carlos Lorca said.

"Carlos," I said, "Morrison has agreed to let me snoop around for King's killer."

"You mean we get to investigate a murder?"

"That's right, except he only agreed to pay me. I knew he wouldn't do it for both of us, so I didn't ask. But you can help anyway. Just go on with your normal routine, but at the same time, find out what you can about King. What did people think about him? Did they like him? Did he have any enemies? Any secrets from the past? See what I mean?"

"Got it."

"And let me know what you find. Okay?"

"Okay." We hung up. Smart boy, Carlos, and eager. In fact, a little too eager at times. I sometimes had to remind him that we weren't on a TV cop show. I even suggested he should throw away his TV set. He didn't do it though. He gave it to his parents, and they threw it away. Unusual people, these Lorcas. They still knew how to read and didn't mind doing it.

I hung around the office the rest of the morning. After lunch I got into my old blue Chevy and drove down to Raven Street. I had some questions for Kathy Dove: Had she seen anyone going into King's office? Did she see anyone leave? Did she see anything suspicious inside or out?

I drove to the 500 block and slowed down. Small frame houses sat on small lawns. I went past 518, 520, 526, 530, and 532. I stopped the car and looked around. Sorry, Scofield. There was no 528 Raven Street. Kathy Dove, how did you get such a convincing driver's license?

I parked the car and got out just to make sure. House 526 sat on the left and 530 on the right. Nothing stood between them, not even a vacant lot. Kathy Dove had sent me out to take the air in front of a phantom house. I couldn't even go inside and tell her mother how sorry I was she'd lost her job.

I went through the process of knocking on a few doors. No one had ever heard of Kathy Dove. Five twenty-eight Raven Street did not exist and never had. I felt lucky that William Morrison wasn't there to see his private-eye dollars at work. He would've put me back on toothpaste duty.

I drove back to the office. As usual, not a whole lot was cooking in downtown Davenport. Factory closings and suburban shopping malls had left much of it as empty as a six-pack after *Monday Night Football*.

Many years before, the city had concocted a grand scheme to revive the area. It would include riverboat gambling on the Mississippi, a convention center, new stores and restaurants, restoration and reuse of historic buildings, and a great deal more. Some of this had subsequently happened, including riverboat gambling, a convention center, and the downtown Morco Drugstore, but most of it remained just a city in the air.

I unlocked the office, sat down, and opened the Quad-City telephone book. No one named Dove lived on Raven Street. The book listed no one named Kathy Dove at all.

I swung around in my swivel chair and stared at the empty red-brick building across the street. The building stood six stories tall. Its features included a decorative cornice, rounded arches over the windows of the top five floors, and retail space on the ground floor. A column of limestone quoins ran up each corner from the ground to the top. A steel fire escape zigzagged down the face of the building from the roof.

I had a lot of questions that day, but the empty building had no answers, so I stood up and walked around the room. Walking around was my main source of exercise. I'd thought about joining a health club, but they wouldn't let me carry my Browning automatic in the weight room.

At four-thirty Carlos walked in. I'd hired him as my assistant after getting the job with Morrison. Two of us could cover more stores and create the illusion that we were actually preventing theft. If I ever lost the account, Carlos would have to go into a different line of work, although I hoped it wouldn't be with a certain drug gang, especially in view of the fact that his parents had previously hired me to drag him away from that same gang.

The parents and I then had to teach Carlos a few civics lessons that he might have learned in high school if he hadn't got kicked out for frequent violations of the rules. Our civics class emphasized the law enforcement, judicial, and penal systems, with special attention given to the penal business. Mom and dad were better teachers than I. Maybe the fact that they both taught in the Moline school system figured into the equation. Connie Lorca taught math, and Roberto taught English. For my part, I offered vivid descriptions of what a felon might encounter in the prisons of Iowa or Illinois.

All this instruction seemed to grab the attention of our young scholar. After Carlos offered many entreaties and made more promises than a politician, the high-school principal gave him one last chance. Carlos returned to school, where his GPA shot skyward. One month after he graduated, I got the job with Morco and Carlos got the job with me.

In some respects, Carlos and I were alike. He had black hair and brown eyes. I had black hair and brown eyes. In other respects, he and I were opposites. He was short. I was tall. He was twenty-one. I was forty-one. He wanted to be a private detective. I wanted to retire.

"How did it go today?" I said. "Anyone confess to King's murder?"

"No, but I did find out a couple of things." He sat down across the desk from me. His blue shirt and khaki pants were neatly pressed. His red tie displayed diagonal rows of soccer balls.

"Let's hear them." I leaned forward, rested my arms on the desk, and waited.

"Two or three people said they'd heard complaints about King. They said some people didn't like him because he was too bossy."

"That's the trouble with bosses," I said, "always too bossy. What else did you find out?"

"I was talking to one of the pharmacists about the murder, and she said it would make Carlotta sad."

"Carlotta? Who the hell is Carlotta?"

"I don't know. I asked the pharmacist, but she wouldn't say. She just smiled and went back to work."

"Very inscrutable, these pharmacists," I said as I leaned back in my chair.

"I asked her again, but she wouldn't say a thing."

"Who was this pharmacist?"

"Linda Byrnes."

"Of course, Linda Byrnes from East Moline, the mysterious East. No hope there. I'll ask around and see what I can find. Anything else to report?"

"Nope. That's it." He leaned back and rested his elbows on the chair's arms.

"Good work, Carlos. Let me ask you something else. You ever hear of someone named Kathy Dove? Young, blond, pretty, not very tall. Has a small birthmark on her right cheek."

He considered this. "No, I don't think so," he said.

"Keep your eyes open. I need to talk to her."

He nodded. "What about?"

"She was in the store right before I found King's body."

"Did you try to find her?"

"Yeah, but she needs a new address. The old one doesn't exist."

Chapter Three

The border between Iowa and Illinois follows the Mississippi River from New Albin in the north to Keokuk in the south. Davenport lies on the Iowa side, at a point where the river flows from east to west. It's one of a cluster of towns and cities, in both Iowa and Illinois, known collectively as the "Quad Cities." In what local promoters grandly refer to as "the metropolitan area," the total population of the Quad Cities approaches four hundred thousand, which makes it larger than St. Paul but smaller than Shanghai.

My family has lived here for a hundred and sixty years. My great-great-grandfather was the first Scofield to arrive. When he got off the train, the first woman he saw was Molly O'Keefe, who'd just arrived from Dublin. My grandfather was a Protestant, but when he saw Molly he instantly converted. Many of their descendants left town over the years in search of what is called a better life. Some found it. Some didn't. Most came back to Davenport.

I'm one of those who never left, and I'm the first private detective in the family. Not everyone in my family approved of this career choice, but I plan to stay in business until I can retire to a park bench overlooking the Mississippi. I have to admit, though, that finding a dead body in a drugstore takes a lot of pleasure out of the job. King's death reminded me of how fragile a human being is.

Two days after the murder, the Morco Drugstore in downtown Davenport reopened for business. I arrived for work a little after nine. I pretended to be looking for shoplifters, but I was really looking for Tracy Gibbs and Brian Walker. Except for King, they were the only employees in the store the night of the murder. Both were working the early shift today. I found Tracy on duty at the cash register. She looked short and dumpy, with bleached-blond hair and a round face. I guessed her age at about forty-two or forty-three. Business was as slow as usual, so I had no trouble getting her attention.

"What did you know about Jason?" I said.

"I didn't know anything about him. He was just another manager." She didn't seem to like the topic. She was probably tired of questions.

"Did you like him?"

"Not really."

"Why not?"

"He always acted polite when other people were around, but when he got me alone, he was real mean." Tracy was warming to the subject. It's easy to hold a grudge against someone, even a corpse.

"Mean in what way?" I said.

"He criticized everything I did. He said I didn't work hard enough. He was always threatening to report me for this or that. He was a real grump." Tracy could be a grump herself, but I didn't point that out. No need to make her compete with a dead man.

An elderly man came up to pay for a jar of Metamucil, and I looked around the store. A teenager wearing a Chicago Bulls cap was putting a bottle of vitamin-E tablets into his pocket.

"Did he treat the other employees like that?" I said after the old man had departed.

"No, just the clerks. He was nice to the pharmacists. They didn't have to take his crap."

"So there must have been plenty of people who disliked him."

"Yes, but not enough to kill him." She had answered what would have been my next question.

The teenager with the Chicago Bulls cap walked up to pay for a candy bar. Tracy took his money and handed him his change. "They say that vitamin E improves your sex life," I said to the kid. He looked at me as if I'd just announced his execution. I was too busy to fool around with a shoplifter, so I said, "Put the bottle back on the shelf and get out." He did it.

I watched him go, then turned back to Tracy. "One other thing," I said.

"Yes?"

"Who's Carlotta?"

"Carlotta who?"

"That's what you're supposed to tell me, Tracy. I haven't worked for Morco as long as you have."

"I don't know. I never heard of her."

"Thanks," I said. I could've said, "Thanks for nothing," but I didn't want to end up with a butcher knife in my chest. Not that I suspected Tracy. I suspected everyone.

I wandered over to the drug counter, where Brian Walker was filling a woman's prescription. She was in a hurry. He wasn't. I looked around the store while waiting for the crisis to end. Like all twenty Morco drugstores, this one sold much more than drugs. The long aisles displayed magazines, make-up, disposable diapers, garbage bags, candles, batteries, DVDs, electric irons, radios, beer, wine, whiskey, various products to relieve hangovers, and a long list of other stuff.

Brian finished filling the woman's prescription, and she walked away. He watched her with his steel-blue eyes until she left. Then he turned toward me and leaned on the counter. He was about the same age as Tracy, but that was their only similarity. His high forehead and Greek nose gave him a regal look you didn't often see in a Morco store. "I hate that woman," he said.

"Why's that?" I said.

"She's always in a hurry. You know what the big rush was this time?"

"No idea."

"She has to mow her grass one last time for the year, and she has to do it in this phase of the moon."

"What phase is that?"

"I don't know, Scofield, but whatever it is, she couldn't wait five minutes for her prescription. She got real nasty about it, and I had to take it because she's a customer."

"Nasty people are hard to live with. How was Jason King as a manager? Was he hard to live with?"

"I had no trouble with him, but I heard the clerks grumbling about him sometimes."

"Why was that?"

"Too bossy, they said. He had a pretty high opinion of himself. I got sick of listening to him brag, but other than that, we got along all right."

"Do you know anyone who might have had it in for him? Any enemies?"

"Not that I'm aware of, but I only saw him at work, and not all that much even then. He stayed in his office most of the time." The phone rang and Brian answered it. He made some notes, hung up, and turned back in my direction, looking curiously at me for a moment. Then he said, "What does all this have to do with the stolen drugs?"

"Stolen drugs?" I said. No one had briefed me on this topic.

"Don't try to kid me," he said. "I know why you spend so much time in this store, and it isn't to catch shoplifters."

"Is that so?"

"Doesn't this murder make you suspect Jason of putting his dirty fingers in the pill bottles?"

"That's certainly a convenient explanation for the problem, especially now that he's dead and can't defend himself." I had summoned enough presence of mind to pretend that I knew what Brian was talking about.

"Convenient for whom?" he said.

"You tell me," I said. He didn't seem to like the implication of this. I wasn't in love with it myself, but I remained adrift, trying to gather more facts about this new revelation. "What do you think Jason did with all those stolen drugs, sell them?"

"What else? Uppers and downers that sell for fifty cents each by prescription bring six dollars apiece on the street."

"I see what you mean," I said, nodding in agreement. "Drugs like that could supplement the cocaine trade."

"Sure could."

Let me ask one last question, Brian."

"Shoot."

"Who's Carlotta?"

He stared at me for a moment, suddenly cautious. "Carlotta who?"

"I asked first, Brian. You tell me."

"The only Carlotta I know is Carlotta Morrison, the boss's wife. Why do you ask?"

"Just wondered. Is she involved in running the business?"

"Not much. She likes to decorate the interiors. She's an artist, you know. She owns a gallery in the Village of East Davenport."

I glanced around the store. From the looks of the yellow and green walls, Carlotta's artistic talent came nowhere close to greatness. "Thanks, Brian," I said. "I'll let you get back to work." He continued to stare at me. I don't think he wanted to get back to work. I think he wanted to find out why I was interested in Carlotta Morrison, but I didn't know why, so I couldn't tell him.

꙳

The Village of East Davenport isn't a distinct village, although it was in the mid-nineteenth century. Today it's simply an area of brick streets and old buildings located in the east end of Davenport. Various contractors have restored the buildings to their original architectural styles, and those buildings now contain a variety of shops and boutiques.

After talking to Tracy Gibbs and Brian Walker, I drove up East River Drive, turned left on Mound Street, drove one block to Eleventh, and turned right. Straight ahead on the left, overlooking Lindsay Park and the Mississippi River, stood the Village Gallery, owned and operated by Carlotta Morrison and undoubtedly subsidized by William Morrison. Art thrives when associated with a chain of twenty drugstores.

I opened the door to the shop, and one of those moronic little bells went ting-a-ling. Two women at the back of the room looked up as I walked in. I immediately saw which one was Carlotta Morrison and which one was her assistant. Carlotta had all the diamonds. The assistant had the broom.

Carlotta started toward me while the other woman went off to stir up the dust. Carlotta was in her early forties, about ten years younger than her husband. She had auburn hair, green eyes, a well-formed nose, a high forehead, full lips, and straight teeth. She looked a little overweight, but only in the right places.

A sweatshop somewhere on the planet had made her dress from something light and bouncy, and she got it bouncing just fine by the time she reached the front of the room. All this bouncing revealed a nice pair of legs. Carlotta smiled as cheerfully as only the rich can smile and said, "Hello, what can I do for you today?"

I thought of something immediately, but decided she didn't mean what I had in mind. Certainly not there in the Village Gallery, where we might knock over a clay pot or kick a hole in an oil painting. "I'm Michael Scofield," I said. "Your husband hired me to provide security in his stores, but right now I'm trying to find out who killed Jason King."

Her smile disappeared faster than a twenty-dollar bill on Friday night. "I see," she said. "What brings you here? Jason wasn't associated with the gallery. He worked in one of the drugstores."

"I understand that, but I thought you might know something about him."

"No, nothing." She crossed her arms and looked at me without a hint of kindness.

"Your name came up the other day. One of your husband's employees was talking about the murder and said it would 'make Carlotta sad.' What do you suppose that meant?"

This startled her, though she tried not to show it. She stared at me a few moments, then said, "I have no idea. Who said it?"

"Someone who must remain nameless. Do you think your husband would know what it meant?" My questions, I confess, sounded about as subtle as a bayonet charge.

"What do you mean by that?" She glared at me.

"You know what I mean. You took biology in high school. Remember? Boy frogs, girl frogs."

"Does my husband know you came here?"

"Not yet. You want to tell him? Give him a call. I'll look up the number for you."

Her tone softened a little. "Why are you doing this?"

"I told you. I'm trying to find out who killed King. All I'm asking you to do is tell me anything you know that might help me."

"I don't know a thing about it." She turned and looked at a vase on a display stand.

"Some of the people King worked with apparently didn't like him. Do you know of anyone who might've disliked him enough to kill him?"

She answered, but with her eyes still on the vase. "No. I barely knew him. I have no idea what other people thought about him." She picked up the vase and examined it as if she'd never seen it before.

"Did he ever mention having any enemies?"

"No."

"Were you sad when he died?"

"I'm sad when anyone dies." She set the vase on the display stand and looked back at me. "Now if you don't mind, I have work to do."

I didn't think she really had work to do, but I might have been wrong. Maybe she intended to wrestle the broom away from her helper. I would've enjoyed watching that, but I'd pushed my luck already, so I took the hint and headed for the door. I thought about ripping the bell off on my way out, but managed to restrain myself.

Chapter Four

The next morning, I drove out to one of the shopping malls on the north side of town. Iowa may lag behind other parts of the country in some respects, but when it comes to shopping malls, ours are as ugly as anyone's. This one was long, low, and gray, with a parking lot the size of a hay field.

I parked my Chevy and walked into the mall, where brass seemed to be the only available metal. The lights suspended from the ceiling gave the central walkway a sickly yellow hue. I walked into the Morco Drugstore.

I never announced my visits in advance. I just dropped in. For security services at Morrison's drugstores, I charged fifty dollars an hour for myself and thirty for Carlos, plus expenses. We performed dangerous work. You never knew when a can of foot powder might explode.

I stood in one of the aisles a couple of minutes, a typical shopper looking for just the right hair tonic. A syrupy orchestral arrangement of a popular song came from an overhead speaker. I walked down another aisle and spotted a young man in blue jeans putting a bottle of aspirin tablets into his pocket. "All right, son," I said loudly. "That's going to cost you a trip to the police station."

"What do you mean?" he said, a startled look on his face.

"I saw you put that bottle in your pocket."

"No, I didn't."

"Yes, you did. Come with me." I grabbed his arm and steered him toward the office in the back. The store was crowded, and everyone in the place stared at us. The kid looked scared. I led him into the office and closed the door.

I sat down behind the desk, and he sat down in a chair facing me. "Good work, Carlos," I said.

"Thanks," he said with a grin. Carlos has perfectly straight teeth, all whiter than ivory.

"Excellent timing, if I may say so. Must be fifty people in the place." Carlos and I had worked this scene many times before. As I always tell my customers, the way to combat shoplifting is to deter it instead of trying to catch people doing it. And you deter it by convincing the potential thief that he or she will probably get caught. That logic explains the purpose of our routine with the aspirin tablets. The people who saw us would tell many others, and the word would get out that Morco Drug had a hot-shot security operation.

The same logic applies to all those video cameras you see in stores. Someone put them there to dissuade you from stealing in the first place, not to catch you in the act of stealing, although that sometimes happens. Security television gets very poor Nielsen ratings.

It's unlikely that anyone is watching the monitors when someone steals a tube of toothpaste, although you might see it after the fact. But even then, how do you find the thief after she leaves? Banks handle all these matters more seriously. Don't try shoplifting in a bank.

I grabbed two paper cups from the top of a filing cabinet and poured a couple of shots of brandy from my utility flask. Pharmacist Dick Pitney walked in. "Company policy forbids drinking on the premises," he said.

"It's a morale-building exercise," I said. "Positive reinforcement for Carlos. Did you see his performance?"

"I did. It was excellent."

"Care to join us?"

"Thanks."

Pitney had a shot. Then he had two more and floated back to his post. Probably gave the next ten customers three pills for the price of one.

I leaned back in the chair and glanced around the office. It reminded me of the office where I'd found Jason King's body: bare white walls, steel furniture, no windows. A jail cell could not have had less charm. "Well, Carlos," I said, "what more do you have on the late J. King?"

"Nothing about King, but I think I found Kathy Dove."

"Good work! Where?"

His face turned red. "The Gentleman's Retreat."

"When was this?"

"Last night."

"Why didn't you call me?"

"It was two o'clock in the morning, Mike, and I wasn't positive anyway. I think she had a birthmark on her right cheek, but she had on a lot of make-up."

"Okay, okay. We'll find out tonight. The Gentleman's Retreat, huh?"

"It was my brother's idea."

"I'll bet."

The Gentleman's Retreat stood on West Third Street in what could be called a neighborhood in transition, the transition being from bad to worse. The block with the Gentleman's Retreat was typical of the area. Several of the old brick buildings on the block were vacant. The rest held taverns, a pawn shop, a second-hand store, a junk dealer, a porn shop, and a hotel that catered to alcoholics. The most memorable thing about the street was the "No Loitering" sign painted on one of the bars. I always found it hard to get a good look at it, though, because of all the drunks standing in front of it.

I parked the Chevy in a vacant lot and walked across the street with Carlos. The Gentleman's Retreat presented a wooden facade where large windows had once displayed hardware and kitchen utensils. The door opened into a small foyer where a guy with short blond hair, thick arms, and a sneer collected the price of admission. I didn't know how I'd record this on my expense account, but I'd think of something.

We walked through the inner door into a large room that smelled of beer and cigarette smoke. The only light turned on protruded from the wall behind the bar, which ran along the left side of the place. The rest of the room was as dark as a coal mine but not as nice.

We felt our way through the darkness to an unclaimed table. We had arrived just in time for the show. I would've liked a beer, but didn't have a signal flare. The light behind the bar went out.

A few seconds later, a beam of light cut through the darkness, illuminating a low stage along the wall opposite the bar. A young woman stood on the stage. She had on a gray fedora, a long trench coat, and black high heels. From somewhere, a recording of a slow jazz number began to play. A saxophone won the decibel contest with the other instruments.

The woman removed the fedora and tossed it aside, permitting her curly blond hair to cascade onto her shoulders. She stood about five feet four inches tall and displayed pale skin, blue eyes, and a small birthmark on her right cheek.

She walked back and forth across the stage a couple of times, then stopped with her back to the wall. She slowly untied the belt around the coat and unbuttoned the buttons. She slid out of the coat and dropped it beside the fedora. Her mother had probably told her a thousand times not to throw her clothes on the floor, but some people never learn. I felt certain that the pile would get larger. If anyone had dropped a pin at that moment, it would've sounded like an I-beam.

She now had on a long-sleeved black dress that buttoned clear up to her delicate white throat, where a white collar suggested purity. The skirt barely reached the top of her thighs, which suggested something other than purity. She wore black high heels, but no stockings. With her back to the audience and her legs straight, she slowly bent down and touched her toes. The gents began to howl.

She stayed in that position a few seconds. Then she straightened up and sashayed slowly back and forth across the stage a couple of times. I could see how she'd landed the job. Her little five-foot four-inch body featured about 70 percent well-formed legs, and the other 30 percent didn't look too bad either.

She finally came to a stop with her back to the wall. Starting at the top, she slowly unbuttoned the dress all the way down to her hard little tummy. The song ended. The woman turned around, gracefully pulled her arms out of the sleeves, let the dress slide to the floor, and kicked it onto the pile with the hat and coat. The howl became even louder.

She turned and walked around the stage a few times to show off her lacy red underwear, then stopped, facing the audience. The bra came off next, slowly, one uplifted breast at a time. Then came the panties, very slowly, a fraction of an inch at a time. A week or two seemed to pass. If the girl was aware of the audience, she didn't show it. But the audience was aware of nothing but her.

She walked around the stage, her eyes downcast, as if looking for something on the floor. She had now taken off everything but her black high-heel shoes, which she apparently intended to leave on. The underwear had somehow found the top of the pile.

She finally stopped in the center of the stage—her legs spread wide apart, her arms reaching out to the front, her head tilted back far enough to let her stare up at heaven. She held this pose for three or four seconds, and the spotlight went out. After twenty seconds of total darkness, the house lights came on. Kathy Dove and all her discarded clothing had disappeared.

The waiters began to circulate again, and the customers returned to their drinks. A lively discussion of the entertainment began. No one was interested in fishing, business, sports, or anything other than the entertainment.

I felt no need to challenge the conventions of West Third Street, so I ordered a Beck's Dark and Carlos ordered a Corona. I know it's unpatriotic to buy foreign beers. I'd buy American brands if they didn't taste like Lake Michigan.

Before the night ended, Carlos and I had tipped the balance of trade well toward Mexico and Germany, respectively. Kathy Dove made two more appearances, and we forced ourselves to watch both. For her second show of the night, she came dressed as a lion tamer, complete with leather boots and a black whip. I won't list the implications of this, but they have little to do with wildlife. For her third and last appearance, Kathy came dressed as a bouncy little cheerleader with a pony tail, pom-poms, and a short pleated skirt. Watching this made me feel so sordid that I had to gulp the remaining beer in my glass to recover.

Carlos and I then made a quick exit and took up our posts—he at the end of the alley leading to the back door, I in the car, engine running, across the street from the front door. Ten minutes later, Carlos called me on his cell phone. "She's coming out with the bouncer," he said.

"Be right there," I said. I drove around to the alley, where Carlos climbed in. Down the way, Kathy Dove and the bouncer were driving off in one of those cars with fat tires. We followed them through the alley, back to Third Street, down Third to Gaines, and across the Centennial Bridge to Rock Island.

They drove downtown and stopped in front of the Sheridan Apartments, a tall brick building that used to be the Sheridan Hotel, back in the days before visitors decided they preferred a motel with a view of an interstate highway instead of a hotel with a view of the Mississippi River. Given a choice between asphalt and water, they'd chosen asphalt.

The bouncer locked the car and went inside with Kathy. Carlos and I waited down the street from the entrance. I would've preferred going inside with Kathy while the bouncer sat in the car with Carlos, but no one gave us that option. An hour later, the bouncer came out and drove back toward the bridge. I couldn't help wondering what they did during that hour. What could you do in that amount of time? Cheer-leading? Lion taming? Life is full of possibilities.

I got out of the Chevy and walked down the street to the Sheridan Apartments. Carlos stayed in the car to watch for the bouncer in case he bounced back on his big tires.

A new desk with a Formica top stood just inside the door to the building. A beefy guard with a brown mustache sat behind the desk. Despite a ketchup stain on the jacket, his blue uniform was his best feature.

"Hi there," I said.

"Yeah," he said.

"I'm here to see Kathy Dove."

"There's no one here by that name."

"She told me to meet her here. She must've just got home."

The guard looked at a large phone console with names and numbers, then back at me. "There's no one here by that name."

He'd said exactly the same thing once before. I didn't like the sound of it any better the second time, so I took a different approach. "Young blond woman. About five-four. Has a small birthmark on her right cheek. Maybe I got her name wrong."

He turned toward the phone console again, but I couldn't tell which name he was looking at. He looked back at me. "Maybe you did."

He made no move to call the elusive Kathy Dove, so I concluded the visit was over and went back outside. The bouncer was nowhere in sight. When I got to the car, Carlos was looking up at the building with my binoculars. In a lighted window on the fourth floor, Kathy Dove was staring out at the darkness. If someone had wanted to kill her, she would've made a perfect target.

Chapter Five

The weekend came and went with no new murders in the Quad Cities. I woke up late Monday morning and had a leisurely breakfast. It's my favorite meal. Sometimes I have breakfast three times a day.

After the bacon and eggs, I carried my second cup of coffee into the living room and looked out the front window. My apartment is on the top floor of an old three-story brick building on Fifth Street in Davenport. On the other side of Fifth, the elevated tracks of the Iowa Interstate Railroad run parallel to the street. Downtown Davenport lies just across the tracks. Beyond that, the Mississippi River flows toward the Gulf of Mexico.

No one ever hears of a small town like mine until a disaster happens. We remember Pompeii only because a volcano buried it. Floods have given Davenport what fame it has. Over the years, most of us have found the cost a little too high. We were satisfied with obscurity, but the river never gave us a choice. The flood of the previous spring and summer had been one of the worst.

A different kind of disaster occurred here in the 1980's, although most people outside the area weren't aware of it. The farm crisis of that decade almost destroyed the farm-equipment industry in the Quad Cities. Factories closed. People lost their jobs. The population of Davenport dropped from 103,000 in 1980 to 95,000 in 1990. The population of the entire Quad-City area fell by 33,000. This crisis, combined with the competition of new shopping centers, had left downtown Davenport dotted with abandoned buildings and vacant lots, many of which I could see from my front window.

I finished the coffee and got dressed. Carlos was already hard at work. I had told him to forget about shoplifters for the morning and keep his eyes on Kathy Dove. He hadn't complained. In fact, he said he'd like to keep his eyes on her for the rest of the year.

I took the Centennial Bridge to Rock Island, pausing halfway across while a maintenance crew went about its work. "How you doing, Mike?" an old high school pal said. "Find any more dead pharmacists?"

"Not yet, Frankie. It's still too early to say."

He motioned to me, and I drove on.

I headed down First Avenue and found Carlos parked a block from the Sheridan Apartments. He was alternately peering through his binoculars and drinking a bottle of mineral water. Kids today will put almost anything into their stomachs. I slid into the front seat beside him. He looked sleepy. "Carlos," I said, "what's the little angel up to today?"

"The bouncer came by about ten and took her to breakfast in Moline."

"Then what?"

"They went to a drugstore. She went inside, and he stayed in the car."

"Of course. First you eat. Then you steal some toothpaste. Was it a Morco store?"

"No."

"Thank God. What happened next?"

"He took her home. Then he left."

"Quite a day, huh? You ready for a break?"

"I guess so." He rubbed his eyes. I went back to my Chevy and Carlos drove home for a nap.

✝

I spent the next three hours drinking coffee from my thermos and counting the bricks on the walls of the Sheridan Apartments. I ran out of coffee before I ran out of bricks. Shortly before two o'clock in the afternoon, a cab pulled up to the door and beeped. Kathy Dove emerged from the building, ran across the sidewalk, and jumped into the back seat. The cab took off and so did I.

A private detective needs all kinds of equipment. One of the most important is a car—and not just any car. It has to be one that won't attract attention. If you want to follow someone, don't do it in a new red Mercedes. Pick a car that's about five years old, dark in color, moderate in price, and average in size—just like most of the other cars on the road.

In my five-year-old dark-blue Chevy, I followed the cab out of Rock Island and into Moline—city of mills. This was Kathy Dove's second trip of the day to Moline. I tried to calculate the significance of this, but nothing came to mind.

The cab pulled up to a new one-story building on Sixth Avenue, and I cruised on past. The sign beside the door said, "Prairie Flower Chiropractic Clinic, Wilson Barber, D.C." I drove around the block and stopped a few doors short of the building. My thermos was empty, so I took a shot of bourbon from my utility flask just to ward off the fever.

Kathy had picked the right place to find a chiropractor. There were plenty of them in the Quad Cities. In fact, the world's first chiropractor began his career in Davenport. On September 18, 1895, David D. Palmer gave Harvey Lillard's spine a firm push in just the right spot, thereby curing seventeen years of deafness.

This success led Palmer to the conviction that all kinds of illnesses could be cured by correcting misalignments of the spine, which he called "subluxations." The idea caught on with a sizable part of the population, and the Palmer School of Chiropractic in Davenport began churning out enough graduates to keep the backbones popping all the way from Minneapolis to Memphis.

I wondered, as I took another sip from my utility flask, what had brought little Kathy Dove into the hands of Dr. Barber. Who wouldn't want to manipulate that beautiful spine? Maybe Kathy had gone deaf wiggling out of her red underwear. Whatever the problem, I wished that Dr. Barber would hurry up. I was out of coffee. It was time for Kathy Dove to put on her clothes and answer some questions.

\

Thirty minutes after Kathy entered the clinic, I spotted a taxicab in the rear-view mirror. It was slowing down. I hopped out of the Chevy and reached the sidewalk in front of the building just as the cab pulled up and Kathy Dove came out the door. "Hi, Kathy," I said. "Back problems?"

She didn't seem to remember me at first. Then a look of recognition crossed her face. Recognition and regret. I stepped between her and the cab. Fortunately, the bouncer wasn't there to clear the way. "I need to talk to you," I said.

"I don't have time," she said. "Get out of the way."

"The police would like to talk to you about your visit to Morco Drug the night Jason King was killed. They'd like to know why you chose exactly that time and place to steal a tube of toothpaste, and frankly, Kathy, I wonder about it, too. I wonder if you did it to get my attention while someone else murdered King. I'll bet Lieutenant Rocco has the same idea. I know where you work and I know where you live, and I don't mind telling. You can talk to me or talk to the police."

The cab driver, a man with red suspenders and an unlit cigar, leaned over and shouted through the open window. "You want a ride or not?"

Kathy Dove looked at the cab, then at me, then back at the cab. "No, I don't need it," she said. The driver muttered a common expletive, and the cab took off.

"You want to talk about it?" I said.

"Not here." She looked around furtively.

"There's a café around the corner."

"Okay."

We walked down the block and around the corner to Marty's Café. Marty was putting a new roll of paper into the cash register. "Hi, Mike," he said. He looked at Kathy, looked back at me, and raised his dark eyebrows. Kathy had just impressed another middle-aged man, and she hadn't even taken off her clothes in front of a spotlight.

She led the way to a booth in the rear. Marty arrived with two menus almost before we did. There's nothing like an attractive young woman to improve service. He put the menus on the table. "How's business, Mike?" he said, looking at Kathy.

I didn't think he was really interested in how business was, but I played along. "Not bad," I said. "How about you?"

He finally looked at me. "Can't complain. People have to eat."

I ordered a cup of coffee, and Kathy ordered a bottle of mineral water with a twist of lime. Little Miss Health and Fitness. She'd probably live to be five or six hundred years old. She had the body for it. Every man within fifty miles could confirm that. Marty returned with our order and walked away.

I put a little cream in my coffee and stirred vigorously. I have to get my exercise somehow. "All right, Kathy," I said, "The Gentleman's Retreat must pay you enough to buy your own toothpaste. What possessed you to lift a tube last Tuesday night at Morco Drug?"

She looked embarrassed. "I'm a kleptomaniac," she said, staring down at the table. "I can't stop myself."

"Sorry, Kathy, wrong explanation. Kleptomania is a rare disease, and I know everyone in the Quad Cities who has it." I didn't really know everyone who had it, but I was trying to get her attention. "Let's start over again. Why did you let yourself get caught stealing a tube of toothpaste at the same time that someone was shoving a butcher knife into Jason King's chest? It looks as if you were trying to distract me. So let's have the truth this time." I was attempting to keep my voice down, but it's hard to intimidate someone quietly.

She looked around. She was afraid of someone, and I knew it wasn't me. So who was it? The bouncer? The police? I assumed the demeanor of a junior-high principal. "Who told you to do it? I want his name, and I want it now."

"He said it was just a joke."

"Who?"

"I don't know his name. He's a skinny drunk with bad teeth. He hangs out in the bars on West Third Street in Davenport."

"That's not much help, Kathy. All the drunks on West Third are skinny and have bad teeth. They won't let you in the bars if you don't look like that. How much did he pay you?"

"A hundred dollars."

"Where would a guy like that get a hundred dollars?" I said.

"He said someone gave it to him to give to me. He was just a go-between." She paused, but I didn't respond. "I'll show you," she said. She reached into her purse and pulled out two fifty dollar bills. "See?"

I nodded and she put the money back into her purse. "What if I had turned you in to the police?" I said.

"The guy who paid me said you were in on the joke. He even told me what to say to you."

This was beginning to sound as if it might be true. I still didn't believe it, but it sounded possible. I looked at my watch. It was almost three-thirty. Too late to go looking for drunks on West Third Street. Most of them would have passed out by now. You wouldn't be able to walk past a bush in that part of town without hearing someone snoring behind it.

After threatening again to expose her to the police, I finally convinced Kathy to drive around with me the next morning in search of the skinny drunk with bad teeth. She also told me her real name was Kathy Linn, but I didn't know whether to believe her or not.

I paid the tab and drove Kathy back to the Sheridan Apartments. I was afraid the bouncer might be there, pulling up fire hydrants just to stay in shape, but he was nowhere in sight.

I walked Kathy inside. The cheerless guard from the night before was again at his post. Someone had tried unsuccessfully to remove the ketchup stain from his jacket. In addition, he now had a mustard stain on one sleeve. He pushed a button that unlocked the door to the apartments. I pulled it open, and Kathy disappeared into the fortress. I let the door close behind her, then turned and gave the guard a toothy grin. "Nice to see you again," I said.

He looked at me as if his life's goal was to put me into a barrel, fill it with cement, and find out how far it would float down the Mississippi. Not very far in all likelihood. I wouldn't make it to New Orleans in time for Mardi Gras. I gave him a friendly wave and walked out.

Chapter Six

The next morning, I drove across the Government Bridge to Arsenal Island and on across the Sylvan Slough to Rock Island. It occurred to me as I turned right on First Avenue that Kathy Dove (A.K.A. Kathy Linn) had chosen a likely town from which to operate her shoplifting operation in the Quad Cities. Rock Island had a long tradition of criminal enterprise. With drug gangs moving into the city from Chicago, that tradition seemed likely to continue.

At nine o'clock I pulled up to the entrance of the Sheridan Apartments. Kathy Dove-Linn kept me waiting for twenty minutes, then came through the door, ran across the sidewalk, and jumped in beside me. She had on dark glasses, a white blouse, shorts, and running shoes. Her blond curls were tied up in a red scarf. She locked the door and pulled down the sun visor.

"Good morning," I said. I wanted our day to start on a cordial note.

"Morning," she said. "Let's go."

I drove across the Centennial Bridge to Davenport. Upstream, the sun reflected off the limestone buildings on Arsenal Island. A towboat was pushing its barges into the lock at Dam 15. Downstream, two diesel locomotives were pulling a freight train across the old steel-truss Crescent Bridge.

We drove down Fourth Street to the west, then cruised slowly back along West Third. "If you see him," I said, "don't point. Just tell me where he is. We don't want to scare him off." My warning proved unnecessary. The skinny drunk with the bad teeth was not on the street. We swung over to Le Claire Park for a quick look, then headed down West River Drive and back to Third Street.

After driving around for an hour, we parked on West Third and pretended to read a copy of the *Chicago Tribune*. After that, we drove around some more. Then we parked again, drove around again, and went to a doughnut shop. I had a doughnut and two cups of coffee. Kathy had a cup of tea. Then we parked on Third Street again. The routine was growing tiresome. "How long do we have to do this?" Kathy said.

"As long as it takes."

"I don't—"

She cut herself off. She was staring down the street. I looked in the same direction and saw the bouncer walking away from a tavern and getting into his car. His appearance had startled little Kathy, and I didn't blame her. He was one scary bag of steroids. His chest, neck, and arm muscles bulged like the tires on his car, and he walked with a menacing stride. But in spite of his threatening appearance, he might have been good looking if it weren't for the unhealthy gray color of his skin and the sneer that habitually contorted his face.

"Who's your friend?" I said.

"Karl Deutsch."

"What's his racket?"

"He's just a guy I know."

After Deutsch drove away, things settled back into the earlier routine. At twelve o'clock, we drove downtown for lunch at Vigo's Café. Vigo's was an old-fashioned beanery with a lunch counter on one side, booths on the other side, and tables in between. A large plate-glass window in front gave the place a cheerful atmosphere. Waitresses with white aprons bustled energetically. Near the door, Vigo surveyed everything from his cash register.

While Kathy freshened up in the ladies' room, I freshened up with two bottles of Beck's Dark. I had two more with lunch and polished off the meal with three cups of coffee. At one-thirty, exactly as planned, Carlos came through the door and sat down at the table.

"Time to change crews and cars," I said to Kathy. "The same man can drive the same car down Third Street only so many times before someone notices the pattern." I turned toward Carlos for agreement, but he didn't notice. He was looking at Kathy as if he would happily give her anything she ever asked for—his car, his money, even his DVD of *The Maltese Falcon*.

I reminded him of his assignment for the afternoon. He nodded in my direction and made some vague noises. I paid the bill and left Kathy and Carlos to find their way out to his car. With luck, he would remember how to turn the steering wheel and push the pedals. He wasn't really in any condition to drive, but after four beers, neither was I.

ϒ

I left the car on the street and walked back to the office. My refrigerator was well stocked with Beck's Dark, just in case of an emergency. I took off my jacket and hung it up. Then I pulled a file folder out of the cabinet and tossed it onto the desk. The desk was an old oak number that my father had bought before such relics became collector's items. I planned to sell it someday and buy a farm.

I sat down at the desk and opened the folder, which contained a copy of the late Jason King's personnel file from the Morco Drug Company. I'd looked at it briefly once before, but I opened it now in hopes of an hour's silence and a sudden revelation. "Saint Michael," they'd call me, "who received a revelation in his office on a quiet day in September." People would come from all over the country and pin dollar bills on my shirt.

King had spent his entire career at Morco, so his file was as thick as a drunk's speech at four in the afternoon. The file revealed these truths: At the time of death, he was forty-three years old. He had two daughters in their teens. He was divorced. He had made sizable contributions to the pension plan.

I fought my way through the folder, pausing along the way to open and drain two more bottles of Beck's Dark. I didn't *have* to drink them. I'm not an alcoholic. I just like to drink. Of course, that's what the guys on West Third Street say.

I turned to a new page in the file and had my revelation. Jason had carried $200,000 in group life insurance, with daughters Jennifer and Jessica named as beneficiaries. This came as no surprise. What did come as a surprise was the additional $200,000 in life insurance that listed Rebecca King as beneficiary, Rebecca being Jason's ex-wife. "Why would he do that?" St. Michael wondered. "Why award all that money to your former spouse?"

I turned another page and had another revelation. Rebecca King was also the beneficiary of Jason's pension plan. Paid in a lump sum, it would give her another $250,000. I swung my chair around and looked out the window at the vacant building across the street. Rebecca King had a $450,000 motive for sticking a butcher knife in Jason's chest. I wondered if she had a good lawyer.

While I had lawyers on my mind, I looked up a number, grabbed the phone, and dialed. "Schwartz and Hancock," a female voice said.

"Let me talk to Hancock," I said.

"May I tell him who's calling?"

"You can tell him if you know." My jokes are so stale that they weren't even funny when Queen Victoria told them.

There was a brief pause. "Is this Mr. Scofield?"

"How'd you guess?"

"They told me about you."

They? Who were *they*? I'd have to hire a detective.

A man's voice came on the line. "Hello, Scofield."

"Hello, Hancock. How are you?"

"Just fine. What can I do for you?"

"They told me at Morco that you were Jason King's lawyer. I didn't think he'd have such poor judgment, but I thought I'd ask."

"It's absolutely true. I can't explain it."

"I'm curious about his will."

"I'll bet you are. So are a lot of other people. Lieutenant Rocco, for one."

"I was wondering why Rebecca was named as the big prize winner."

"Sorry, Scofield. I want to stay in business."

"It seems strange that he left her anything at all."

"Does it?"

"With their being divorced, I mean."

"I don't know, Scofield. I wouldn't want to say."

"Let me put it another way. I first assumed he hadn't left her a dime. Should a person make assumptions like that, Hancock?"

He hesitated. "Not necessarily."

"Not necessarily?"

"That's what I said, and that's all I'm going to say. So don't ask me any more questions."

"Got it."

"And don't confuse my new secretary with your old jokes. It's already hard enough to find someone who can type these days. In fact, it's hard to find someone who can sharpen a pencil."

"Sorry. I'm sick with remorse."

"You should be. Goodbye."

"Goodbye."

After talking to Hancock, I called cashier Tracy Gibbs and asked her about the problem of the missing drugs at the downtown Morco. She blamed it on Jason King, then began complaining about the way he had treated her. I'd heard that story before, so I thanked her and hung up, and not a minute too soon. The sound of her whining voice echoed in my head for ten minutes.

At three o'clock, I put on my jacket, locked the door on the way out, and headed for the stairs. That's when I noticed a large object in the middle of the hallway. I stopped for a closer look. The object was Karl Deutsch.

"Where's Kathy?" he said.

"Kathy who?" I said.

"You know who I mean. I saw you driving around with her this morning."

"That's very good. The steroids must have improved your eyesight."

"Where is she?"

"But they didn't improve your IQ."

That got him moving. He came at me as fast as he could. I stepped forward and gave him two left jabs in the nose. Blood splattered his face and shirt. He stopped a moment, surprised, then backed up to regroup.

Deutsch was slow-witted and muscle-bound, but I'm no Muhammad Ali. I'm not even Gorgeous George. And I'd just wrecked a six-pack of Beck's Dark, something Angelo Dundee always told his fighters not to do right before a big match.

Now revived, Deutsch went on the offensive again with wild swings from both his left and right. I worked on his nose and eyebrows, opening cuts above both eyes. His face was covered with blood. Angelo was yelling at me to keep my guard up and go for his belly. I was thinking about how good another beer would taste when one of Deutsch's roundhouse rights caught me in the temple and made me wish I'd gone into the real-estate business.

I was calculating the advantages of a career change when a left hit me in the forehead and dropped me to the floor. I took a mandatory eight count and stood up. It was a big mistake. Another blow struck me and I took another eight count. I started to get up again, but the floor grabbed me and pulled me back down. Something hit me in the body two or three times and I lost count. Never was much good at math. Then something hit me in the head, and I went to sleep.

Chapter Seven

It was a short nap. I picked myself up and staggered back into the office, where I collapsed into my chair and imagined a world in which I'd never been born. I took out my handkerchief and wiped the blood away from my eyes. When my strength began to return, I picked up the phone and called a cab.

The folks in the emergency room at St. Luke's Hospital checked me out for broken bones and damaged organs. Once they realized I wasn't seriously hurt, they made far too many jokes about tough-guy private detectives. They sewed up a couple of wounds on my head and said they wanted to keep me under observation for a couple of hours. I told them I'd had enough of their observations and headed for the door.

A cab took me back to my car, and I drove home. I watched my step when I got there. I didn't need any more jokes from the comedy club at the emergency room. I looked around before getting out of the car and kept my eyes open while walking into the building. Mr. Weaver, an elderly black neighbor on the first floor, stuck his head out and asked me how I was. I said I felt like shit. Then I corrected myself. I felt worse than shit. He took me into his apartment and gave me a shot of apricot brandy, and I began to feel better.

The two flights of stairs up to my floor were longer than they had been that morning. When I finally got into my apartment, I filled a plastic bag with ice and lay down on the floor. The phone rang. I crawled over and picked it up, dragging the ice behind me. "Scofield," I said. I found the sound of my own name comforting. It added credibility to the theory that I was still alive.

"Mike." It was young Carlos. His voice had the ring of success. "Kathy and I found the drunk who gave her the hundred dollars. We followed him back to where he lives."

"Where's that?"

"In a vacant building on West Third, not far from the Gentleman's Retreat."

"Okay, we'll have to catch him in the morning while he's still sober. Where's Kathy?"

"I took her home."

"Good."

"You don't sound so hot, Mike. You okay?"

"I'll live. But if you see Deutsch, do me a favor."

"What's that?"

"Run over him."

⸸

At seven o'clock the next morning, Carlos and I were sitting in my car outside the former home of the Kiner Monument Works. My head didn't hurt as much as the night before, but the rest of me felt much worse. I hoped that Deutsch felt the same.

We waited for a while, but the skinny drunk with bad teeth did not emerge from the monument works. So we got out of the car and went into the building through a broken door in back. I wanted to pick out a tombstone for Deutsch. It would have to be a big one.

In the dim light of the back room, we saw a man lying in a corner. "Hello," I said. The man didn't move. You find a lot of heavy sleepers on West Third.

As we walked over to the corner, a feeling of dread hit me in the guts. This guy was sleeping too soundly, even for this neighborhood. I took out my pocket flashlight and turned it on. The first thing I noticed was the way he stared into the light. The second thing was the Gerhart-Brooks butcher knife sticking out of his chest.

I kneeled down and felt his throat. His skin was cold, his pulse still. "Is this the man Kathy identified?" I asked as I looked at the body.

"Yes," Carlos said. His voice quavered just a little. Looking for shoplifters hadn't prepared him for this. Nothing could.

I stood up and looked at Carlos. "You didn't see anyone follow him in here last night, did you?"

"No."

"He's been dead several hours."

"Yeah."

Carlos didn't look too well. "You'd better keep watch outside while I look around here," I said.

Carlos walked out, and I gave the place the once-over. I knew that when the cops arrived they wouldn't let me near the body. I checked the dead man's pockets for identification. He didn't have any. What he did have was a broken comb, a pocketknife, and one thousand dollars in cash. It was the money that caught my attention. How would a homeless drunk get that much cash? I looked around the room, but found nothing else.

I went outside and told Carlos to call the police. He took out his cell phone and hit the buttons for 911. The first cop arrived in two minutes. Before long the place was full of them. They closed off the area with long strips of yellow plastic and talked to each other on their radios. I stood around and waited for some higher being to bring order out of chaos. Five minutes later, the higher being arrived.

"Lieutenant Rocco, good morning," I said.

"Do you mind telling me what you were doing here?" he said.

"Looking for shoplifters." I escorted him into the back room. He turned on his flashlight and stared at the dead man.

"You didn't touch the body, did you?" he said.

"Of course not."

"You noticed the knife, I suppose."

"Yeah. Another eighteen-dollar Gerhart-Brooks butcher knife. Someone got his money's worth." My ex-wife used to tell me I used humor in inappropriate situations. This was one of many things we disagreed on.

"So why did someone use the same kind of knife used on Jason King?" Rocco asked, even though he already knew the answer.

"Looks like we might have a madman at work, doesn't it?"

"Yes," he said, staring at the body. "God help us if we do." He scratched his chin, then his cheek.

"Yeah."

"Do you know who the dead guy is?"

"No, I was hoping you could tell me."

"What happened to you, by the way?" he said, turning in my direction. "You look like hell."

"I stubbed my toe."

He grunted at me and walked away, and I concluded the interview was over. I went outside, where another detective was questioning Carlos. I told Carlos to call me later. Then I took off.

The dead man was just another faceless alcoholic. Like any other town, Davenport had its share of them. It also had some who weren't so faceless.

The town's most famous alcoholic was undoubtedly Leon "Bix" Beiderbecke. He was born in Davenport in 1903 and grew up in a big house on Grand Avenue, where he fell in love with jazz. Later, he fell in love with alcohol, which eventually killed him at the age of twenty-eight. If you go to the Oakdale Cemetery in Davenport, you can easily find his grave. If you look a little farther, you can also find the grave of the homeless alcoholic who died many years later at the Kiner Monument Works.

✝

There's nothing like a visit to West Third Street to make a guy long for East Third Street, so I put my aching body behind the wheel of my Chevy and headed east. As usual, downtown Davenport was about as busy as an iceberg. I parked on the street and walked into Vigo's Café, where I had a cup of coffee and a sweet roll. Caffeine and sugar are crucial to the healing process.

Vigo left his spot by the cash register and walked along the counter to where I was sitting. He had a large stomach, a large nose, and black hair flecked with gray. "You don't look so good, Mike," he said.

"I don't feel so good," I said.

"What happened?"

"I made friends with a guy named Karl Deutsch."

"The body builder?"

"Yeah."

"You picked the wrong playmate."

"You said it."

Vigo refilled my coffee cup and walked back to the cash register. I finished the second cup, then strolled over to my office and listened to the messages on the answering machine. None of them promised me money or pleasure, so I erased them. After that, I called Kathy Dove-Linn, who had kindly given me her number the day before. Calling was much easier than waiting outside her apartment in hopes she might come out.

"I have some bad news," I said. "The man who gave you the hundred dollars has finished his last bottle of Thunderbird."

"What do you mean?"

"He's dead, murdered."

"Oh dear." She actually sounded sad.

"Do you have any idea who might have killed him?"

"No."

"Are you sure?"

"I'm sure."

I waited a couple of seconds. "If you hear anything about it, let me know."

"I will," she said, but I didn't have much confidence that she would.

"I had a visit from your boyfriend last night."

"What boyfriend?"

"Karl Deutsch. He wasn't very friendly. You don't know what was eating him, do you?"

"I think he was worried about me. He usually picks me up on Tuesday to go shopping, but yesterday I was still with Carlos. I'm sorry."

"Thanks. I feel much better. You don't suppose he had anything to do with the drunk's murder, do you?"

"No. Why would he?"

"Good question. Did he finally catch up with you yesterday?"

"Yes. He took me to work and drove me home afterwards."

"How did he look?"

"Pretty bad. His nose and lips were swollen and he had stitches above both eyes. He said he ran into something."

"He did. Me. Do you think he'll recover?"

"Yes, I think so."

"Sorry to hear it."

Two dead bodies. Not a good score for the Scofield Detective Agency. Every time I made an appearance, someone ended up with eighteen dollars worth of stainless steel in his chest. I'd have to take the word "security" out of my promotional literature, if I ever had enough money to print any.

I waited until afternoon to call Rocco. "What do you want?" he said at the other end of the line. I noticed a hint of irritation in his voice.

"I know it'll be in the papers tomorrow, but I'm in a hurry. Who was the dead guy I found this morning?"

"Joseph Meiers. He had a long list of arrests for alcohol-related crimes in Moline and Rock Island before he started hanging out on this side of the river a couple of years ago." Rocco's tone had mellowed a little. He actually liked me, but pretended not to sometimes.

"Were there any prints on the knife?"

"No, it was wiped clean, just like the one used on Jason King."

"How old was Meiers?"

"Forty-two."

"Just a baby. What did he do for money?"

"Not much. He swept up at the Gentleman's Retreat once in a while. You might also be interested in knowing that he worked for your boss's wife occasionally." I could hear Rocco scratching his chin.

"You mean the lovely Carlotta?" I said.

"The same," Rocco said.

"I doubt if she pays top wages."

"Probably not."

"So how did he come up with a thousand dollars?"

"I thought you said you didn't touch the body."

"Sorry."

"I'll overlook it this time if you'll let me know anything you find out."

"Sure. I can tell you right now that Jason King and Carlotta Morrison were especially close."

"Is that right?"

"Sure is. All roads lead to Carlotta."

✶

It was late afternoon by the time I pulled up to Carlotta Morrison's art gallery in the Village of East Davenport. The trees in Lindsay Park were holding up their fistfuls of red and yellow leaves. Beyond the park the Mississippi was showing the peaceful side of its personality.

As I walked across the street to the gallery, I decided to modify my interviewing technique. I hadn't gotten to first base during my previous visit. I hadn't even gotten into the ballpark. The bell tinkled as I walked in, and Carlotta met me at the front of the room. She was wearing a blue suit, a white blouse, and black high heels—the uniform of the ideal businesswoman. There was no one else in the shop. "Hello, Mrs. Morrison," I said.

"Hello," she said. She stood with her arms crossed.

"I hope you don't mind my bothering you again. It's just that Jason King's case has taken a new turn, and I was hoping you could help me."

"I don't see how, but go ahead if you must." She was still cool. Time to turn on the Scofield charm.

"One of the customers in the store that night was paid to go there and distract me. The man who paid her was Joseph Meiers." A look of recognition crossed Carlotta's face. I forged ahead. "When I found Meiers this morning, he was dead, murdered the same way as Jason King."

"Oh no," she said. Her hands dropped to her sides. Her concern seemed genuine.

"I'm afraid so. I understand he used to work for you."

"Yes. He was kind of a handyman, though not a very good one. And he helped clean up sometimes. He wasn't very dependable though. He was an alcoholic. Sometimes he wouldn't show up when he was supposed to."

"Did you fire him?"

"No. I just learned not to depend on him too much."

"Why so generous?"

"I felt sorry for him. He was a good person. He meant well." She looked away.

"Do you have any idea who might have wanted to kill him?"

"No," she said, looking back at me. "I can't imagine who would do such a thing. He was a gentle person. I doubt if he had an enemy in the world."

"He had at least one."

"I guess he did."

"He also had a thousand dollars on him, which means robbery wasn't the motive."

"A thousand dollars?" She stared at me, a surprised look on her face.

"Yeah. Strange, isn't it? Can you think of any way he might have come up with that much money?"

"No, he always looked destitute when I saw him. I had to feed him sometimes before he could work. Last winter I let him sleep in the storage room sometimes because he had nowhere else to go."

This was a philanthropic side of Carlotta I hadn't noticed before, although I had noticed before how attractive she was. Today she seemed even more attractive. The blue suit accented her auburn hair, which fell in a long wave onto her shoulders. Her clear green eyes had taken on a new softness. "Look," I said, "I'm sorry I got a little cute the last time with the stuff about Jason. It was only a rumor started by a disgruntled employee."

"Actually, it wasn't a rumor. It was true. I just didn't like your manner."

"I was only bluffing when I said I'd talk to your husband about it."

"It wouldn't matter if you did."

"Why not?"

"He doesn't care."

"Really?"

"Yes, really. He's gay."

"He is?" I was surprised and made no effort to hide it.

"Yes. He doesn't care what I do as long as I'm discreet."

I saw my chance. "How discreet do you feel right now?" I said.

She looked at me a moment, a playful smile forming on her lips. "You don't waste time, do you?" she said.

"Time is too valuable to waste." I gave her what I hoped was a winning smile.

"You wouldn't waste my time, would you?"

"Absolutely not." I shook my head solemnly. She crossed her arms and looked me over from top to bottom. I tried to appear relaxed. She took her time and didn't complain about what she saw.

Finally, she strolled over to the door, locked it, and pulled the shade. Then she strolled back to me, hips swaying gently, stopping just inches away, so close that I felt the warmth of her breath. She placed her forefinger on the side of my chin.

"Right now, I feel very discreet," she said.

Chapter Eight

Having an affair with someone else's wife isn't such a smart idea, especially with your boss's wife. It's better to stay home with your own wife, if you have one. I don't.

I used to have one, but we didn't get along. She wanted to live in an expensive box in the suburbs, and I wanted to live in an apartment overlooking a brick street and a railroad track. When we broke up, she got the box and I got the track. I couldn't imagine a better settlement.

Before the divorce became final, I quit my job and announced to the world the birth of the Scofield Detective Agency. The world barely noticed. In the first year, I earned less than half of what I earned the previous year selling computers. I spent most of my time that first year spying on unfaithful spouses, when I was lucky enough to have a job at all. This was a little vulgar for my taste, but I couldn't afford to be proud. At least I didn't have to go home to a mortgaged house and a two-car garage.

When they erected the apartment building I live in now, they didn't have two-car garages. They didn't have garages at all. People walked or took the trolley. The invention of the automobile led directly to garages, large houses, and divorces. That's Scofield's Law. Look it up if you don't believe me.

The morning after my visit with Carlotta Morrison, I drove down to West Third Street and parked the Chevy. My ribs still ached from Deutsch's kicks and Carlotta's embrace. I hoped that no one on West Third would want to give me a hug.

I began with a visit to Betty's Tap. The room was long, narrow, and dark, with booths on one side and the bar on the other. The bar stools looked a little wobbly, just the way I felt, so I stayed on my feet. A guy in a baggy old suit was sitting at the end of the bar closest to the door. He needed a haircut, a shave, and, most of all, a bath.

I leaned on the bar and asked the guy what he was drinking. He was obviously drinking wine, but when he saw my coat and tie, he immediately switched to straight whiskey with a beer chaser. I ordered a round for him and a glass of orange juice and three aspirin tablets for myself.

I waited for him to finish the booze. I wanted him to feel grateful before I asked any questions. The man wasted no time. He gulped the whiskey, drained the beer, and looked hopefully in my direction. "You didn't happen to know Joseph Meiers, did you?" I said.

"Sure, I knew him. Everyone did." He gestured vaguely with his right hand, as if the whole world lived on West Third Street.

"Do you have any idea who killed him?"

"No, no idea. You a cop?"

"Private investigator. Michael Scofield."

"It figures. The cops won't pay for whiskey, just cheap wine."

"Meiers had a lot of money on him when he died. Where do you suppose he got it?"

The man hesitated. He looked sadly at the empty glasses in front of him. "Sorry, I don't know anything about it," he said. "I gotta go." Before I could say another word, he slid off the stool and headed for the door. Two other guys got up and moved away from me, to the other end of the bar.

No one else at Betty's wanted to talk to me. They wouldn't even let me buy them a drink. I finally walked out the door and down the street to Red's Place. My performance there duplicated the one at Betty's. By the time I got to Harv's Tavern at the end of the block, no one would even say hello. News of my coming had preceded me. I began to wonder if all the drunks on West Third had email. I crossed the street and worked my way back down the block on that side. No luck. I finally gave up. I was willing to pay, but the only thing I could buy was orange juice.

※

I climbed into the car and drove downtown. The coffee still tasted good at Vigo's Café. Vigo reached across his big belly and filled the cup. He wouldn't take my money for coffee. He was still grateful that I had helped him sandbag the place during the spring flood.

I went on over to the office and opened the windows. Then I leaned back in my chair to think. I didn't think about Jason King or Joseph Meiers or the man in the baggy suit. I thought about Carlotta Morrison.

Carlotta had two of the nicest legs I'd seen in quite a while. I wondered how long I should wait before taking another look. I didn't want to appear too eager. If I showed up at her gallery every day, I might have to start sweeping the floor.

I was still thinking about this when the phone rang. "Scofield Detective Agency," I said.

"Are you the guy who was asking questions about Joe Meiers this morning?" a woman said. She spoke with a faint rasp, so faint I had a hard time hearing her. The rasp was the kind you get after decades of cigarette smoking.

"Yes, I was in a few bars on West Third Street, but nobody wanted to talk to me."

"They're all scared. I'm scared, too, but Joe was a friend of mine. I want someone to catch the guy who killed him."

"What can you tell me?"

"I know where he got the money."

"Go on." I picked up a pencil and grabbed a piece of paper.

"A guy got him to file a damage report with the government after the flood last spring. He gave Joe a house address and told him to say he rented the place. And he told him what losses to claim—furniture, clothes, and stuff like that."

"Who was this guy?"

"Max Brady. He owns the Marquette Hotel." The Marquette was a small firetrap on West Third.

"So the government paid Joe a thousand dollars to cover his losses."

"It actually paid ten thousand, but Joe only got a thousand."

"Why?"

"Brady had him list the Marquette Hotel as his temporary address after the house was flooded. When the check came, Brady got Joe to sign it. Then Brady cashed it himself and gave Joe the thousand."

"And kept the rest for himself."

"That's right."

"Did Joe ever actually stay at the Marquette?"

"No, that was just part of the scam, like everything else about the whole deal."

"So who killed Joe?"

"I don't know."

"Brady?"

"Maybe. Maybe not."

"Why's everyone afraid to talk about it?"

"Joe wasn't the only one who filed a phony claim for Brady. There were others. They're afraid of getting caught or getting killed."

"Who are they?"

"I don't know. Joe just said there were others."

"How many?"

"I don't know. I don't think he knew either."

"Do you know the house address Brady told him to use?"

"Yeah. One twenty-nine Rose Street. Joe and I went down to look at the house just as a joke."

"Who owns it? Brady?"

"I don't know."

"What else can you tell me?"

"That's about it."

"Where can I reach you if I need to?" I knew better than to ask for her name.

"You can't. If I find out anything more, I'll call you. Goodbye."

I attempted to keep her on the line, but she hung up. I tried to match her voice with the women I'd seen in the bars that morning, but I couldn't make a connection. Maybe she'd call again.

I looked at the address I'd written down, 129 Rose Street. I pulled my copy of *Polk's Davenport City Directory* out of a drawer and looked up the address. The house was listed as vacant. I checked the other houses on that block. Some listed occupants, but most were vacant. Carlotta would have to wait. I had to take a drive.

　　　　　　　　　　ϯ

Rose Street runs north and south through the most flood-prone residential section of town, a west-side area of about eight square blocks known as the River Village Addition. The addition was built to alleviate a housing shortage among factory workers during the prosperous war years of the 1940's. It's a neighborhood of small frame houses on small lots. During the flood of the previous spring, half the houses in the River Village Addition had been under water.

The house that had brought Joseph Meiers an easy thousand dollars sat on the block of Rose Street closest to the river. The only man-made objects standing between it and the Mississippi were West River Drive and the Soo Line Railroad, neither of which would hold back a bowl of gravy.

I found 129 Rose Street, parked at the curb, and got out. The house looked like the type that people all over the country were trying to get away from. It had been cheaply and poorly constructed to begin with, and now the flood had turned it into something like a mud hut. I walked across the cluttered yard and peeked through the window in the door. The front room contained two broken chairs, a ruined couch, and a TV set with a hole in the center. No one had made any attempt to clean up the mud that covered everything, including the walls, up to a height of about three feet.

I walked around to the back and looked in a window. The kitchen contained a small refrigerator, a gas stove, a table and chairs, and assorted junk. The refrigerator door stood open. A dead carp lay on the bottom shelf. If someone from the Federal Emergency Management Agency had come out to take a look, he or she would have seen plenty of damage, and it would not have been clear how long the house had been vacant. Mud hides all kinds of evidence.

I walked back to the sidewalk, although it was difficult to tell exactly where the mud on the lawn ended and the mud on the sidewalk began. I looked up and down the street and counted the houses on both sides of that block. There were twelve. Only one appeared to be occupied. I walked over and knocked, but no one came to the door. This didn't surprise me. People in the River Village Addition had to work for a living.

I had started to walk back to the Chevy when a squad car pulled up in front of the house and a man in uniform got out. "Excuse me, sir," he said with official politeness. "Could I see some identification."

I showed him the ID card the Iowa Department of Public Safety issues to private investigators. The cop didn't look impressed. "What are you doing here?" he asked.

"I was looking for someone at one twenty-nine Rose, but it appears to be empty. I'm following up a lead for a client in a shoplifting case." It's better to keep things simple when dealing with the cops. If they think you're interfering with police business, such as a murder investigation, they'll give you a lot of gas, and it won't make your car run smoothly.

The cop handed back my ID. "People in this neighborhood are worried about looters," he said, "so we're keeping an eye on things."

I got the hint. "I was about to leave," I said. I walked to the Chevy and climbed in. The cop watched as I drove off. I glanced at him several times in the rear-view mirror. He watched me all the way to Rockingham Road.

֏

I drove back down Rockingham, past the factories and packing plants where the people of the West End worked. East of the City Cemetery, Rockingham Road curved slightly and joined West Second Street. After a few blocks on West Second, I turned left, drove a block to West Third, and stopped in front of the Marquette Hotel.

The Marquette had never been a luxury hotel, and a quick look told you it never would be. It was a simple three-story brick building on a corner lot, with the entrance opening onto Third Street. The building used to have a metal cornice, but when it grew old and threatened to fall off, the owner found it cheaper to remove it than to repair it. The residents didn't care one way or the other. Architectural flourishes meant nothing to them. All they wanted were four walls, plenty of cheap wine, and a bed to pass out on.

I walked through the door and across the small, dark lobby to the desk. The flood hadn't reached the Marquette, but the place looked dirty enough anyway. In fact, a flood might have made it look cleaner. The man at the desk was thin and partially bald. The hair he still had was black and oily. He was wearing baggy pants, a white shirt, and a clip-on bow tie. On West Third the tie looked elegant. "May I help you?" he said with perfect indifference. What he really wanted to do was help me turn around and get out.

"I'm looking for Max Brady," I said.

"So am I."

"Oh, really? Why?"

"He owes me two weeks back pay."

"Does he have an office somewhere?"

"Not that I know of."

"Where does he live?"

"I don't know."

I was starting to realize that this desk clerk didn't know a whole lot. "What about a phone?"

"He doesn't answer."

"But it's still connected?"

"Yeah." He tapped the edge of the counter with a pencil.

"Where's he from? Maybe he went home to see mom and dad."

The clerk stopped tapping and gave me a weary look. "I doubt it," he said. "He told me one time that he grew up in Carlton, Illinois, but I don't know. He never mentioned his family."

"What does he look like?"

"Why are you looking for someone if you don't even know what he looks like? You don't even know him, do you?"

"I'm a private investigator hired to find him. He just inherited two million dollars."

"Oh yeah?" This was the first time the clerk had shown any real interest in our conversation. "Well, he has blond hair, blue eyes, a droopy mustache. Average in height and weight. Between forty and forty-five years old. Two million, huh?"

"That's right. Could I have your name?"

"Sure. Fred Hutz."

I wrote it down, then skillfully changed the subject. "You have many flood victims staying here?"

The clerk gave me a long, hard look. "I don't know," he said. "I don't ask about things like that."

"Just wondered. You're not too far here from the part of town that got hurt the most."

"Far enough."

"Someone might stay here until he came up with the money to clean his place up."

"Someone might stay anywhere he wanted to. Now if you don't have anymore questions, I have things to do." He started tapping the counter with the pencil again.

I had a lot more questions, but I could tell that standing around the lobby of the Marquette Hotel would get me nothing but flat feet. So I walked out to the Chevy and drove away.

Chapter Nine

If you look out my front window, as I do every morning after breakfast, you can see three of the six bridges that cross the Mississippi in the Quad Cities. On the left, the 1895 Government Bridge carries cars, trucks, trains, and pedestrians from Davenport to Arsenal Island, where three small bridges cross the Sylvan Slough to the Illinois shore. When the Government Bridge was still new, hundreds of people walked across it every day to work at the arsenal. I rarely see anyone walking across it now. We're all too much in love with our cars.

On the right, as you look out my window, the five arches of the Centennial Bridge join Davenport and Rock Island. My friend Louie used to collect tolls on this bridge, but the State of Illinois eliminated the tolls and the toll-talker in 2003. I don't know what Louie does now. On the far right, the Crescent Bridge carries rail traffic across the river.

Prostitution has long been a major industry in Davenport. By the year that I went to work for Morco, prostitution had moved to "The Row," the block of West Third Street between Gaines and Brown, where illegal drugs also contributed to the retail mix. During a one-day sting operation that year, the police arrested sixty-three citizens for attempting to buy drugs or sex from undercover officers. You never knew what to expect on West Third.

The morning after my visit to the Marquette Hotel, I finished my daily survey of the city from the front window and took my empty coffee cup back to the kitchen, where I called Rebecca King, Jason King's ex-wife. She said she'd be happy to see me. There's nothing like a $450,000 death settlement to encourage sociability. I shaved, dressed, put on a red tie, and went down to the car. My wounds had started to heal, and I felt almost presentable.

Rebecca King lived in a treeless suburb north of the city, not far from the treeless suburb where my ex-wife lived. I pulled up in front of her house and got out of the car. A Nissan Sentra with a long scratch on the side sat in the driveway. The lawn revealed the extensive use of herbicides. Red geraniums grew in a straight line along the front of the house.

Rebecca King met me at the front door. She was about the same age as Carlotta, but that was the only thing they had in common. Rebecca's hips were wider and her thighs thicker. She had dark circles under her eyes and the odor of cigarettes on her breath. She was wearing white slacks and a plaid blouse. When she smiled, her make-up cracked like a layer of ice on a warm day in February.

She showed me into her living room and offered me a beer, which I declined. I never drink before noon. She offered me coffee, which I accepted. She motioned toward a long white couch, and I sat down. When she returned with coffee for me and a beer for herself, she sat down at the opposite end of the couch and smiled at me again. "What did you want to see me about?" she said. She lit a cigarette and filled the room with deadly blue smoke.

"As I mentioned on the phone, I'm looking into the murder of your former husband."

"Uh-huh." She was waiting for me to get to the good part.

"I wondered if you had any idea about who might have killed him."

"No, no idea at all. I hadn't seen him for ages. We were divorced fifteen years ago, and our paths didn't cross much after that." She puffed on the cigarette and tapped it on an ashtray.

"Do you remember if he ever mentioned having any enemies, anyone who might have had it in for him?"

"No, Jason wasn't usually the kind of person to make enemies. He kept his opinions to himself and went out of his way to act friendly to everyone. This was just a facade, of course, but most people didn't know it." She took a slurp of beer. I took a sip of coffee. It tasted like the stuff you use to unstop drains. I set the coffee on an end table to let it evaporate.

"Why do you say it was just a facade?" I asked.

"He didn't like everyone as much as he pretended. He just acted that way to get ahead in business. When his guard was down, he showed his real personality."

"Why did you get a divorce?"

"I wondered when you'd ask that." She sucked more smoke into her lungs and exhaled slowly. "We got a divorce because he had an affair with another woman. It started almost as soon as we got married. I didn't know about it for a long time, but when I found out, I told him he had to end the affair or I'd divorce him. He chose the divorce."

"Who was the other woman?"

"Mr. Scofield, if you don't already know that by now, you're not much of a detective."

"I want to hear it from you. Other people will tell you all kinds of stories. I never assume anything."

"Carlotta Morrison, the whore."

"What happened with them after the divorce?"

"She played him along. I don't know if they ever really broke it off. Jason had the stupid idea that she would leave Morrison and marry him, but I knew she'd never do that. She loved her husband's money too much. She'd never dump him for someone else unless he had more money. That's all she cares about, that and screwing every man who walks in the door. "This judgment was hitting close to home. I tried not to blush. "Jason was a sap to think she'd ever marry him." Rebecca flicked her ashes toward the ashtray but missed. The ashes disappeared into the fabric of the thick gray carpet.

"I noticed in Jason's personnel file that in addition to your daughters, he also named you as a beneficiary for his life insurance. Why did he do that?"

"It was part of the divorce settlement, nothing more, nothing less. We both knew there would be expenses with the girls, and we wanted to make sure the money would be there if it was needed. I didn't kill him for the insurance money if that's what you're thinking."

"I'm not thinking anything. I'm just looking for answers. I don't suspect anyone." I smiled as I uttered this lie. I suspected her and everyone else.

"Jason was a sap, and I hated him for what he did, but I never would have killed him."

"Of course not."

"He was such a fool. Carlotta never dreamed of marrying him, not even after he got her pregnant."

"Pregnant?"

"That's right. Didn't know about that, did you?" She smirked. She was enjoying this.

"No."

"Not many people do."

"Did she have the baby?"

"Apparently."

"What happened to it?"

"I don't know. When the pregnancy started to show, Carlotta took a long vacation somewhere in the East. When she came back she wasn't pregnant anymore. Morrison didn't care. He doesn't care what she does as long as she keeps it quiet. He's a fag."

"So she must have given the baby up for adoption."

"I guess so."

"When did you find out about all this?"

"A few years later. I figured out what was going on and confronted Jason. He told me, the stupid shit."

"Was the baby a boy or a girl?"

"I don't know. I don't think Jason knew either. Pretty strange, huh?"

"You said it." I pondered this for a moment, then changed the subject. "Someone has been stealing drugs from the downtown Morco," I said. "Do you think Jason was involved?"

"I doubt it," she said. "Jason would fuck every whore in town, but he wouldn't steal drugs. Too risky." She paused. "Would you like a beer now?"

"Yes." I suddenly felt very thirsty. My rule against drinking before noon underwent immediate revision.

She left her cigarette smoking in the ashtray, went into the kitchen, and came back with a can of something from Milwaukee. I wanted to tell her about the miracle of German beer, but I repressed the impulse. She had given me a lot of information, and I didn't want to appear ungrateful. Of course, everything she'd told me could have been a lie. People love to lie even more than they love to drink. Some people don't drink at all, but everyone lies. Believe me.

She handed me the beer and sat down again, much closer this time. She drank from her can and I drank from mine. I could tell that she was already half loaded, and I now suspected that she wasn't the one who tended the lawn. You have to be able to stand up in order to push a lawn mower. She inched a little closer, and

I started to get nervous. "Would you like to stay for lunch?" she said.

I thought fast. "I'd love to," I said, "but I have an appointment in Chicago."

"That's too bad," she said. She lit another cigarette and blew smoke in my face. "Maybe some other time."

"Sure," I said. I coughed three or four times and smiled weakly. "Some other time." I gulped half the beer and made my escape. On the way out to the car, I met a delivery man. I thought about warning him, but decided against it. Maybe he'd have time for lunch.

Chapter Ten

I left the delivery man to his fate and drove downtown to my office. The air was crisp, the sky blue. It was one of those fall days they would have called "glorious" in the nineteenth century, but glory had long since fled the Quad Cities. The best we could hope for was a day without toxic spills.

I climbed the steps to the second floor and unlocked my office. It was still as small as the day before. I listened to the answering machine and erased the messages. Why do people always want my money? Do they think I'm a rock star?

I opened the mail, all of which was junk, and threw it away. Then I picked up the phone and called Carlos at the Muscatine Morco. He said he'd just caught a young man trying to steal a toaster. It was the bulge under the guy's jacket that gave him away.

I started typing a report of recent activities and expenses for Morrison. Someday maybe I'd have a secretary to do that sort of thing. Someday maybe the Mississippi would turn into Beck's Dark. That would change everyone's opinion of floods.

The National Guard would be called in to tear down the levees. Volunteers would stay up all night emptying sandbags.

After twenty minutes of hunting and pecking, I pushed away from the typewriter and got out my city directory. I wanted to talk to Max Brady, owner of the Marquette Hotel and alleged disaster-fraud artist. Maybe there was a connection between him and the murders. Maybe there wasn't. Either way, I had to find out.

The directory listed an address on Clay Street, on the bluff overlooking the old working-class neighborhood known as the West End. The West End included both West Third Street and the Marquette Hotel. I wrote down Brady's house number, turned the answering machine back on, and went down to the car.

Brady lived in an old, well-maintained brick cottage. In a block of large houses, his was the only small one. I parked at the curb and walked to the door. No one came when I pushed the button. No one came when I knocked. I walked over to a window and peeked in. The room looked dark, tidy, and fully furnished. I walked around to the back door and peered into the kitchen. Refrigerator, stove, table, chairs, counters, and cupboards all gleamed back at me. The calendar on the wall displayed the correct year and month. Brady might have been out for the day or out for the year, but the little house seemed to expect him back.

I stepped away from the door and walked over to the one-car garage. There was no car in it, but plenty of other stuff was—rakes, a lawn mower, a garden hose, shovels. A nice quiet garage. I walked back to the Chevy and drove downtown to City Hall.

The Davenport City Hall is a limestone building constructed in 1895 in the Romanesque style of architect H. H. Richardson: round arches, a rough-stone exterior, towers and turrets, massive scale. Unlike many of today's buildings, City Hall was built to last.

Only one clerk was on duty in the Assessor's Office. She kept me waiting five minutes while she completed some official business on the phone with her mother. Finally, she hung up. "What can I do for you?" she said.

"I'd like to see the records for the River Village Addition," I said.

The woman frowned as she lifted herself out of the chair. It couldn't have been easy. She was dangerously overweight. She trudged over to a cabinet, searched through it, and found what she was looking for. Nothing was too much trouble for our public servants. She carried the records over, put them on the counter, and returned to her desk.

I started looking, expecting to find Max Brady listed as the owner of 129 Rose Street. I wondered what other properties he owned in the River Village Addition. My mysterious female informant had said that others besides Joe Meiers had worked the flood-damage scam. I wanted to get an idea of how extensive the racket might have been.

The information I found raised more questions than answers. The records listed River Village Enterprises, not Max Brady, as the owner of 129 Rose. In fact, the records listed River Village Enterprises as the owner of every inch of property in the eight-square-block area closest to the river. Was Brady the owner of this firm? If so, he'd acquired a large portion of the least desirable real estate in town. But the records gave no clues about ownership of the company. They listed only "George Mann, general manager."

"Excuse me," I said to the clerk.

She looked up from a copy of *People* as if I'd just cut off her arm. "Yes?" she said.

"I just looked up a property in the River Village Addition that I thought was owned by Max Brady, but the records list River Village Enterprises. Do you have any information about that?"

The clerk closed her magazine with a sigh. "Some property down there changed hands recently," she said. "Let me help you." She struggled to her feet again and eventually arrived at the counter. She had clearly resigned herself to the fact that she would have to help me in order to get rid of me.

What she found came as a complete surprise. River Village Enterprises had purchased the eight square blocks in question only a few weeks before, long after the flood. The seller of the entire mess was the very busy Mr. Max Brady. With the clerk's help, I found that Brady had bought up the area, house by house and lot by lot, over a period of about five years. The amounts paid had varied, but all had been low. Real estate values had not fully recovered from the farm crisis and factory closings of the 1980's, and Brady had swooped in just in time.

I had one final question. "Who owns River Village Enterprises?" I said.

"I don't know."

"Does Max Brady have an interest in it?" I knew that smart operators sometimes sold properties to themselves in order to avoid public scrutiny.

"I don't know," she repeated. "All the records say is 'George Mann, general manager.'"

I wrote down the address and phone number for George Mann and left the clerk to return to her duties. As I walked out, she sat down at her desk and picked up the magazine.

After lunch, I made an unscheduled visit to George Mann, general manager of the shadowy River Village Enterprises. His office was on the tenth floor of the Empire Building in downtown Davenport. The Empire Building was erected in 1927, before architects discovered glass. A smooth-faced limestone exterior covered the building's steel frame. The building stood eleven stories high, with a clock tower at the summit. It was one of the most elegant structures in town. If the Scofield Detective Agency ever made enough money, I planned to move into the Empire Building. The lobby where you waited for the elevator was, by itself, six times larger than my office at Fourth and Brady.

The sign on Mann's door said, "Property Management Associates." The secretary was wearing a red dress and a string of pearls. Her hair was dark and her eyes blue. The "associates" didn't rush out to meet me, so I asked to speak to Mann himself. The secretary asked if I had an appointment. "No," I said, "but I'd like to schedule one for two o'clock this afternoon."

She looked at her watch. "It's already two o'clock," she said with the assurance of someone who has just discovered an absolute truth. The experience brought new color to her cheeks. She was young and pretty, but not as pretty as she thought.

"I know," I said. "That's why I want to schedule the appointment for two. I'm already here."

This confused her. She looked at her watch again and then at the phone.

I said, "If you'd like to schedule it for five after two, I'll be happy to go out and come in again."

She picked up the phone and pushed a button. "There's a man here to see you," she said. She listened a moment, then looked up at me. "May I have your name, please."

"Mike Scofield. I'm a private investigator."

The secretary spoke into the phone again, then hung up. "Mr. Mann will see you now," she said.

"Thanks." I walked around her desk and through the door.

Mann had a large office with a dark-red carpet and a mahogany desk. The window behind him overlooked a block of downtown buildings, with LeClaire Park and the Mississippi River beyond. On the wall to my left hung a watercolor painting of Lock and Dam 15. On my right, built-in bookshelves held a small TV set, assorted trinkets, pictures of people in power boats, and a copy of the Iowa Code.

Mann stood up, shook hands, and motioned toward a chair. He wore eyeglasses and appeared to be in his late forties. His wavy, brown hair parted on the left. His features, though not ugly, were undistinguished. He had on a blue pinstripe suit, which authorized him to conduct business anywhere between Boston and Reno. Special rules applied in California.

"What can I do for you today?" he said after sitting down.

"I was looking at a house in the River Village Addition the other day," I said.

"Oh?" he said cautiously. Putting on a pinstripe suit always elevates a man's rating on the caution index.

"It's the house at one twenty-nine Rose Street. I found out at the Assessor's Office that it's owned by River Village Enterprises."

"Yes." More caution.

"It listed you as general manager."

"That's correct." At last, a commitment. "I do manage that property for River Village Enterprises. I'm afraid, though, that it's not on the market, if that's what you had in mind."

"No, actually, I'm conducting an investigation that has led me to a man named Max Brady. He owned the property previously."

"That's correct." If Brady's name worried Mann in any way, he didn't show it.

"In fact, I discovered that Brady owned all the properties down there that were subsequently purchased by River Village Enterprises. I was wondering what Brady's current connection with that company might be. Is he the owner, or one of the owners?"

"Well, now, that's something I couldn't say. The owner or owners don't wish to be identified at this time."

"Why not?"

"Mr. Scofield, as a businessman I'm sure you know that business can be very competitive. Businessmen may not want the competition to know their plans."

"How many owners are there?"

"At least one." He smiled. There it was again. Old Mr. Caution. "Perhaps if you told me who your client was, I might be able to help."

"Sorry. He doesn't wish to be identified." This wasn't entirely true, but I enjoyed saying it.

"In that case, I don't see how I can help you any further."

That was my cue to stand up and get out, but I wasn't quite ready. "It seems odd to me that Max Brady happened to buy many properties that River Village Enterprises later happened to buy from him. Somebody knew what somebody else was going to do. Doesn't that seem odd?"

"I really couldn't say, Mr. Scofield." His smile had dissolved. I couldn't think of any more questions. So I stood up and made my exit. The members of the "Enterprises" were still missing. I wondered where they hung out. Maybe in one of the mud-filled houses in the River Village Addition. I left Mann's office, smiled at the secretary, and walked out.

꠸

Back in my office at Fourth and Brady, I called the Secretary of State's office in Des Moines. I stated the purpose of my call, and in a few seconds a woman came on the line. "How can I help you?" she said.

"I'm conducting an investigation that's led me to a firm called River Village Enterprises," I said. "I haven't had any luck here in finding out who owns it. I was hoping you could look it up for me."

"Certainly. I could look it up and call you back. How does that sound?"

"That sounds just fine." I gave her my number, thanked her, and hung up.

I paced for a few minutes, then sat down at my desk to do some work. Two hours later, the woman called back. Things were moving at lightning speed in state government that afternoon. "What did you find?" I said.

"River Village Enterprises is wholly owned by the Davenport Development Company," she said.

"Any names associated with this outfit?"

"Just one, George Mann, president."

"You're kidding."

"I'm afraid not."

"But George Mann is the general manager of River Village Enterprises," I said.

"I noticed," she said. "I thought you'd want to know, so I went ahead and looked up the owner of the Davenport Development Company. It's wholly owned by Riverfront Properties of Rock Island, Illinois."

"I'm almost afraid to ask. Who owns Riverfront Properties?"

"I don't know. You'd have to call Springfield for that."

"This could go on forever."

"At least."

"Thanks anyway. You've been swell."

"You're very welcome."

It didn't take the intellect of Immanuel Kant to see that the owner or owners of the River Village houses did not want to be found. All that a call to Springfield would get me was a phone bill. Besides that, it was already five o'clock on Friday afternoon.

I locked the office, walked down to the car, and drove back to Brady's house on Clay Street. I retraced my steps from that morning, hoping that Brady might have returned. After looking through both the front and rear doors, I headed back toward the front, not sure what to do next.

As I walked around the corner of the house, I almost ran into a man headed in the opposite direction. I stopped abruptly and took a step back. The sun was shining in my eyes, but I could still see well enough to tell who the man was. "Karl Deutsch!" I said. "How nice to see you again."

Chapter Eleven

I stepped to the left to get the sun out of my eyes. Deutsch scowled at me. His complexion was pale, his eyes dull. The sneer on his lips looked congenital.

"What're you doing here, asshole?" he said. I noted with pleasure the stitches above his eyebrows.

"My name isn't asshole," I said. "You must have me confused with someone else."

"I don't think so. What're you doing here?"

"I'm looking for Max Brady. What're you doing here?"

"I'm looking after things."

"Is he out of town?"

"That's none of your business," he said. His fists were clenched.

"Of course it is," I said. "Max is an old friend of mine. We took the same correspondence course in hotel-motel management. How do you happen to know him?"

"That's none of your business either."

"Is it possible that he owns the Gentleman's Retreat as well as the Marquette Hotel? That would explain it, wouldn't it?"

"Maybe he does. Maybe he doesn't." Some of the bite had gone out of Deutsch's voice, suggesting that I'd stumbled onto the truth.

"I'll bet you do all kinds of work for my old friend Max. What do you know about the eight square blocks of the River Village Addition that he just sold to River Village Enterprises?"

"Get out."

"That's not very friendly. Max will be disappointed in you when I tell him how you snubbed a fellow hotel-motel manager."

"Get out!"

"I don't think so, Karl. I think I'll stay right here and wait for good old Max."

As he started toward me, I reached for the holster under my jacket, pulled out my Browning automatic, and pointed it at his chest. Perfect timing. Deutsch retreated several feet. I backed up, waited a moment, and started to return the pistol to its holster. No need to alarm the neighbors. This proved too much of a temptation for Deutsch. He stepped forward again and swung at my head with his right hand. I ducked, straightened up, and flattened his nose with a left jab.

He backed up, shook it off, and came at me again. I feinted with my left and hit him in the belly with my right. The gun was still in my hand, so the blow carried extra emphasis. The Marquess of Queensberry would not have approved, but you can't please everyone. Deutsch didn't care about the Marquess or anyone else by then. He was lying on the ground trying to breathe.

I was tempted to kick him a few times, as he'd done to me, but I didn't want the word to get out that I was a common thug. It takes years to build a good reputation. So I put the automatic back into the holster and headed for the car. I didn't want to be around when the bell sounded for round two.

ϒ

I drove home and drank a bottle of Beck's Dark to celebrate my victory in the Scofield-Deutsch rematch. I figured my share of the gate plus T-shirt sales would net me at least five or six million.

I opened another bottle and peered into the fridge. Scofield needed food before going out for another street brawl. Maybe a nice piece of raw meat would do. There wasn't any in the fridge, so I settled for a couple of poached eggs on toast, a glass of milk, and a pot of coffee. I hate to cook. So did my wife. TV dinners and a mortgaged house. What a marriage.

After dinner I put the dishes into the dishwasher and drank my third cup of coffee. Then I made a phone call. "Gentleman's Retreat," a man's voice said.

"This is Max," I said.

"Max! Where you been? You coming in tonight?"

"No, not tonight."

"Fred just called to see if you were back."

"Fred who?"

"Fred from the hotel. What other Fred is there?"

"Oh, yeah. That Fred." An image of the desk clerk formed in my mind.

"Yeah, that Fred. This isn't really Max at all, is it?"

"Sure, it is. I—" The line went dead. Max needed to train his employees in correct telephone etiquette if he wanted to stay in business. West Third Street had its reputation to maintain. I put down the phone and poured another cup of coffee.

\

It was getting dark by seven o'clock. I parked across the street and a few doors down from the Gentleman's Retreat. Perhaps Max Brady would make a surprise appearance. I hoped so. After a few minutes, a middle-aged man hurried up to the door and walked in. A minute later a man in blue jeans and a cap went in. Two college boys arrived next. Other people continued to dribble in for the next hour.

At about eight, Karl Deutsch and Kathy Dove-Linn came walking around the corner and went through the front door. He was sort of hunched over, as if he might have an upset tummy. He knew my car by now, but gave no indication that he saw me. A few minutes later, he came back out, walked down the street, and disappeared around the corner. I waited five minutes, but he didn't come back.

I hopped out of the car and trotted across the street to the front door. A new bouncer took my money and let me in. I walked over to the bar and ordered a beer. When the barman returned I said, "Is Karl here tonight?"

"Karl?" he said. "No, you just missed him. He left about five minutes ago. Said he had a stomachache."

I resisted the temptation to slap my knee and laugh out loud. Instead, I said, "How about Max?"

"No, he's not here either."

I drank my beer, then went back out to the car. I sat there awhile in hopes of learning something else, whatever it might be.

Finally, a young woman in high heels and a short, tight skirt walked down the sidewalk to my car and bent down to look in the open window on the passenger's side. She had green eyes, an intelligent face, and plenty of make-up. "Hi, sugar," she said. "Looking for something?"

I gave her a big smile. "No thanks, officer," I said. "But have a nice night."

Chapter Twelve

Monday morning, after surveying the world from my front window, I called Springfield. The woman who spoke to me wasn't as cordial as the woman in Des Moines, perhaps because I let it drop that I was calling from out of state. I couldn't vote in Illinois. I didn't pay taxes in Illinois. What good was I?

After a lengthy delay, the woman called back and reported that Riverfront Properties, Rock Island (owner of the Davenport Development Company, which was the owner of River Village Enterprises), was wholly owned by the Great River Company, also of Rock Island, Albert Vox, president. The woman said that Albert Vox lived at the Sheridan Apartments, number 510, in Rock Island. I couldn't help noticing that this was the same building Kathy Dove lived in.

I found the number, picked up the phone, and dialed.

"Hello," said an elderly male voice.

"Mr. Vox?"

"What?"

"Is this Mr. Vox?" I spoke louder.

"Yes."

"Mr. Vox, this is Michael Scofield. I'm a private investigator here in the Quad Cities. The state of Illinois has hired me to trace the owners of uncollected income tax refunds, and your name is on the list."

"Oh?" His voice became more youthful. Money does that to people.

"That's right. I wondered if I might be able to meet with you this morning to verify your identity." He told me to come right over.

The guard at the door was the same one who'd been so helpful when I was trying to find Kathy Dove-Linn. A new food spot had joined the other spots on his blue jacket. "What do you want?" he said.

"I have an appointment with Mr. Vox," I said. I smiled cheerfully, but he didn't smile back. I don't think he believed me. He looked up the number and dialed. He spoke to someone, hung up, and looked at me as if I had created a new volcano across the street.

"Go on in, hotshot," he said. Unlocking the door for me may have been the most painful event of his life.

"Thank you," I said. A soft answer turneth away wrath.

I took the elevator to the fifth floor, walked down the hall, and knocked at 510. The man who opened the door looked even older than the voice on the phone. He was at least ninety. His hair was white, his eyes gray, his teeth false. He was tall and lean and moved about as fast as a mountain range.

He led me to a couple of rocking chairs and we sat down. The room was furnished with antiques, some of which may have been as old as Mr. Vox. "What's this about the money?" he said.

"As an officer of the Great River Company, you're eligible for an income-tax refund for the last year. Could you tell me how long you've been president of the company?"

"Been what?"

"President." I talked louder.

"Present what?"

"Aren't you the president of the Great River Company?"

"What great company?"

The interview wasn't going well. I took a new approach. Speaking very slowly, I shouted, "Do you own any property in Davenport?"

"In Davenport? No." He looked at me as if the very idea was a felony.

"Do you know Kathy Dove?"

"Kathy Dove? No."

"Kathy Linn?"

"No."

We were really cooking now. I moved ahead. "Do you know Karl Deutsch?"

"No." The rhythm was hitting new highs. I leaned forward.

"Max Brady?"

"No."

"Joe Meiers?"

"No."

"George Mann?"

"George?"

"Yes. George Mann. Do you know him?"

"I know George."

"How do you know him?"

"I know George," he repeated. "George is my grandson."

I sat back in the chair and started to rock. "Thank you, Mr. Vox," I said. "That's all the questions I have today."

"Do I get the money?"

"No, I'm afraid not." I stopped rocking and stood up. "Only one refund to a family." Before he had time to reflect on this, I said goodbye and walked out.

⸸

It was a dirty trick to fool an old guy like that. I felt guilty, but not for long. I took the stairs down to the fourth floor, walked along the hall to apartment 414, and knocked. Kathy Dove-Linn arrived at the door in a bathrobe and, I suspected, nothing else. It wasn't as becoming as the trench coat or as provocative as the cheerleader's outfit, but the day was still young. Plenty of time to put on and take off a closet full of clothes.

"What do you want?" she said.

"I need to talk to you," I said as I looked over her shoulder. I was prepared to change my plans if I saw Deutsch.

"How'd you get in? The guard didn't call me."

"That's true, but don't blame him. I came here to see someone else, and once inside I thought I'd drop in on you."

"How did you know what room I was in?"

"I looked at the guard's list as I went past his desk. Poor security procedures here. I'll have to call the management and offer my services."

I had worked my way into the apartment by now. She closed the door, sat down on a white couch, and picked up a lighted cigarette from an ashtray. I considered telling her that cheerleaders shouldn't smoke. It projected the wrong image to children.

"What do you want?" she repeated. She didn't invite me to sit down, but I did anyway, in a white easy chair with its back to the wall. A detective has to guard his rear if he wants to stay out of the hospital.

All the furniture in the room was white, including the end table beside the couch. A painting of a white sailboat hung on one wall. A large mirror in a white frame hung on the opposite wall. A big white television set stood across the room from the couch. I saw no books, magazines, or newspapers.

"What do you know about Max Brady?" I said.

"I know that he owns the Gentleman's Retreat and he owes me two weeks pay. Do you know where he is?"

She suddenly seemed more happy to see me. Maybe she thought I knew where Max had gone with her back pay. "I have an idea where he might be." This wasn't true, but I didn't want to lose her attention. "Maybe I can help you." Another lie. "What do you know about his purchase and sale of properties in the River Village Addition?"

Blankness settled on her pretty little face. "What do you mean?"

"Brady bought and sold dozens of houses down there. Do you know anything about it?"

"No."

"Before he sold them, he had people filing flood claims for personal losses in those houses, even though most of them were probably vacant. People like Joe Meiers. I think your boss is taking everyone he can to the cleaners, and you're just the latest. He may have even killed Joe Meiers to cover up his disaster fraud and God knows what else. And he probably killed Jason King, too. Why don't you tell me what you know about him." I couldn't think of any reason why Brady would have murdered King, but I didn't mention that problem to Kathy.

"I don't know anything." She snuffed out her cigarette in the ashtray and lit another one. She looked nervous. I didn't know whether to believe her or not.

"What about Karl Deutsch?"

Her eyes met mine, then darted away. "He works for Brady. That's all I know."

"That's all? How can you spend so much time with him and know so little. I thought he was your boyfriend."

She suddenly laughed, a reaction I hadn't expected. "What's so funny?" I said.

"He's not my boyfriend. He's my bodyguard. Sometimes men try to follow me home or pick me up. Brady told him to keep the weirdos away."

I knew it would be fruitless to point out that the Gentleman's Retreat was the last place to go if you wanted to avoid weirdos. "Do you think Deutsch knows where Brady is?"

"He might, but he wouldn't tell me if he did. He doesn't tell anybody anything."

"Probably not. He's too busy thinking."

She looked at me, then laughed again. And in spite of myself, I laughed with her.

I didn't put much faith in Kathy's word. I suspected that she knew more about Max Brady than she admitted. Deutsch was Brady's boy, and Deutsch looked after Kathy. She had to know something. All this talk about back pay might be just a smoke screen to make everyone think Brady had left town. Fred Hutz, the desk clerk at the Marquette Hotel, had told the same sad tale. They all probably knew where Brady was, and I was probably a lot closer to home than they wanted me to think. They knew it was a good idea to lie low after cheating the feds. The feds might want their money back.

The situation called for bold new measures. I went back to the office and got on the phone. "Carlos," I said, "I'm pulling you out of the stores for a while. I have a new assignment for you."

"What is it?"

"I want you to follow Kathy day and night, watch everything she does, write down everywhere she goes. I think she knows more about Max Brady than she admits. Do you think you can handle it?"

"Do I? I mean I do, I can." The boy was eager. Confused but eager. He'd follow Kathy Dove-Linn through a downspout if he had to.

"Don't get careless. Watch out for Deutsch, and keep me informed. Got it?"

"You got it. I mean I got it." Still confused, but he'd calm down. Mention of Kathy Dove-Linn had induced temporary hysteria. He'd come out of it. I said goodbye and hung up.

Chapter Thirteen

After putting Carlos on the trail of Kathy Dove-Linn, I went to lunch. I allowed myself three beers, which lowered my normal inhibitions and prompted an early visit to the lovely Carlotta.

The bell went ting-a-ling when I walked in, but it didn't bother me. With three beers under my holster, not much did. Carlotta was talking to a customer, so I wandered around the shop, looking at the merchandise. The selection included a number of nonrepresentational paintings and sculptures, meaning that each piece looked like nothing or looked like everything, depending on the perceptions of the viewer.

The walls of the gallery were uniformly cream colored. The oak floor glowed beneath multiple coats of polyurethane. Lights dangled at various angles from metal tracks attached to the ceiling.

The customer finally made her purchase and left with a small painting under her arm. Carlotta put the check into the cash drawer and walked over to me with a smile on her face. Commerce brought joy to Carlotta like nothing else. Almost nothing else.

She stopped two feet in front of me. We were the only ones in the store. I stepped forward and rubbed against her. She rubbed back. "How's business?" I said.

"Very good," she said. Her perfume smelled like a flower shop.

"Want to close early?"

"Not this early."

"That's too bad." I got ready to pout.

"How about tonight?"

"Tonight would be just fine." No need to pout after all.

"Nine o'clock at your place?"

"See you then." I kissed her lips. "Bring your legs."

⟨

She arrived at exactly nine. We Midwesterners are known for our punctuality. This is only one sign of our moral superiority. Straight teeth and clean underwear are two other signs. I forget the rest. Carlotta smiled at me when I opened the door. Her teeth were definitely straight, and I was eager to check her underwear. I'd planned for lengthy preliminaries: drinks, food, soft music. Forget it, Scofield. Carlotta did not require such stimulants.

Afterwards, we stood at my front window, looking out at the lighted buildings of downtown Davenport. Beyond the buildings, the Mississippi River glowed in the moonlight. An unhurried succession of headlights came across the Centennial Bridge.

Carlotta drank a martini and I had a beer. She smoked a cigarette, although she was trying to quit and was down to three a day. I had quit five years before and was glad of it. Smoking was bad for your health, and I needed to be in top condition for my next match with Deutsch. My body had pretty much healed by now, and I wanted to keep it that way.

"This is a nice view," Carlotta said.

"I like it, too," I said. "I grew up on Cork Hill, which isn't a bad place to live, but this has a better view."

"It's lovely," she said. "Lovely" is a word you don't hear much anymore. It belongs, like "glorious," to an earlier, more innocent time.

"I like it here. Even with street gangs, it's better than the suburbs. And I can keep your husband's drugstore in view in case someone tries to walk out with a cash register under his raincoat."

"How's the murder investigation going?"

"I've run into a dead end with a guy named Max Brady. He owns the Marquette Hotel and the Gentleman's Retreat. Joe Meiers worked for him sometimes. You don't happen to know him do you?"

"No."

"I need to ask him some questions, but he's disappeared."

"Too bad."

"Then there's a young woman named Kathy Dove, or sometimes Kathy Linn. She knows more than she's telling. She's a stripper at the Gent's Retreat. You don't know her, do you?"

"I don't think so," she said. "I don't hang out there." She kissed me. "Sorry I can't be more help."

"That's all right," I said. She put her hand between my legs. "That's all right," I repeated.

An hour later, I walked Carlotta down to her car, and she headed back to the security of her husband's fortune, leaving me satisfied but still ignorant. If she couldn't answer my questions, who could? Nobody. Absolutely nobody. I looked at my watch. It was eleven o'clock, time for direct action.

I went back upstairs and packed my tools. Then I walked down to the car, drove to Clay Street, and parked under the dark canopy of an oak tree. I watched Brady's house for twenty minutes. Nothing happened. Nothing moved. I got out of the car.

After walking quickly and silently down the sidewalk, I cut through the yard and around to the back door. Here I stopped and waited another minute. No sign of life inside or out.

I took out the duct tape and put a series of strips on the bottom window pane in the door. Then I put on a pair of leather gloves, wrapped a towel around my hand and wrist, and poked a hole in the glass. I removed the towel and pulled out the taped glass. Then I reached through and unlocked the door. This method of investigation was admittedly crude, but judges didn't give search warrants to private eyes.

I turned on my flashlight and walked through the house until I found a desk. It had three drawers on each side and a wide, shallow drawer in the middle. For the next twenty minutes I carefully went through each drawer. I stopped occasionally to listen for footsteps. I was afraid of the police and even more afraid of Karl Deutsch.

By the time I was ready to go, I had sorted through piles of bills, typing paper, notebooks, envelopes, photographs, pencils, pens, paper clips, and other junk. In the midst of all this, I found two useful items. The first was a picture of a man who matched the description of Brady given to me by the hotel clerk: blond hair, blue eyes, droopy mustache. The second was a bill listing Brady's Mastercard number. I also found a stack of girlie magazines, but I didn't have time to sit down and enjoy them.

I quickly searched the rest of the house, but found nothing useful. Finally, I went through the garbage. It's not something I like to do, but we all have to sacrifice to create a better world. In a wastebasket in the kitchen, I found another bill, this one with a Visa number and the name Max Burns.

I gathered up all my stuff, left the house in a mess, and walked innocently back to the car, a good citizen out for a moonlight stroll. By one-thirty I was back in my apartment, drinking a beer and looking out over the city. I had hoped to find a signed confession at the house on Clay Street, but you can't have everything. One way or another, I had to find Max Brady.

Chapter Fourteen

I called Carlos at nine o'clock the next morning. He was already in his car, parked outside the Sheridan Apartments. The boy loves his work. Kathy Dove-Linn had not yet made her first appearance of the day, and Carlos's tone suggested that he was eager to see her. I told him to call me if something developed.

I hung up and went down to the car. Fred Hutz, the desk clerk at the Marquette Hotel, had told me that Max Brady claimed to be from Carlton, Illinois. I had no reason to believe either Brady or Hutz, but the time had come to check it out.

Carlton stands on the Illinois prairie fifty miles southeast of the Quad Cities. I drove down in about an hour, arriving at eleven o'clock. I'm a careful driver. Whatever the speed limit is, that's how fast I drive. My ex-wife drove like Mario Andretti at the Indy 500, but all she ever won were speeding tickets. She never did much of anything during our marriage, but she was always in a hurry to do it.

Carlton looked like most of the other small rural towns in the Middle West. Half the commercial buildings on the town square stood empty. "For Sale" signs littered the yards in residential areas. The streets were as quiet as a monastery. The people who still lived in Carlton now drove their cars to the Wal-Mart on the edge of town or to the nearest shopping mall. And they drove there on excellent roads. Businesses failed, farms went broke, and the population declined, but the witnesses to this disaster still had the best roads in the world.

I drove straight to the police station a block from the town square. It was a small brick building next to the city hall. I parked the car and walked inside. When you're working in a strange town, it's always best to check in with the local police before you start snooping around. Inside the building, I found two people, a secretary and the chief of police. Without having to count the chief's patrolmen, I knew how many he had: four. Just enough to keep one cop on duty at all hours, with one working the days off for the other three. The secretary was a luxury not all small towns could afford.

The chief was a big man, which had probably been his main qualification when he became a cop three or four decades before. He had gray hair, a broad face, and a double chin. He had a double stomach, too. I showed him my ID. Then I showed him the picture of Max Brady I'd stolen the night before.

"Have you ever seen this man?" I said. "He goes by the name Max Brady or Max Burns. I need to talk to him in connection with a fraud investigation." I didn't mention anything about the two murders. The police don't like to see private cops involved in police business. It makes them nervous. "He claims that Carlton is his hometown."

The chief took the photo and stared at it. "No, I don't recognize this face," he said. "Is this a recent picture?"

"I think so. If he grew up here, he probably left about twenty-five years ago, assuming he left right after high school."

He returned the photo and looked at me carefully. "What kind of fraud?" he asked.

"Filing false claims with FEMA for flood damage."

"Then why aren't the feds involved? That's their jurisdiction, isn't it?"

"That's true, but I'm trying to build a case before turning it over to them."

If he believed this, he didn't show it. "How long you gonna be in town?" he said.

"Just today. Thanks for your help." I turned and headed for the door. I could feel his eyes boring into the back of my skull. If he was trying to read my mind, I hoped he wouldn't read the part about the broken window in Max Brady's back door.

I got into the Chevy and drove back to the town square, where I found a public telephone beside a dilapidated bandstand. The phone was in a real phone booth with a door that opened and closed. Small-town life still held some charm. Inside the booth I found a phone book that was largely unmutilated. I flipped to the "B's." The book listed no one named Brady or Burns in Carlton or the surrounding area. Things were not looking all that promising for the Scofield Detective Agency.

As I climbed back into the Chevy, a city patrol car drove slowly by. The cop behind the wheel looked at me as if I were Vito Corleone putting a dead horse in someone's bed. He had apparently heard from the chief, and he had his orders.

I drove to the high school, which stood on the east side of town. Yellow school buses lined the street out front. The parking lot was full of foreign cars. I parked the Chevy and got out just as the police car came cruising by. The cop was ready to stop me the moment I started sawing down the flagpole.

The cornerstone for the three-story brick building gave the date 1927. In 1927 the people of Carlton could not have imagined what would happen to their little town. I wondered how long it would be before the school was shut down by a consolidation scheme. When that happened, Carlton would lose its last reason to exist.

I walked into the school and found the wood-paneled offices of the principal and the superintendent of schools. Neither they nor their secretaries had worked for the school district more than ten years. So I wasn't surprised when they didn't recognize my photograph of Brady. The principal suggested that I talk to Alice Moyer, the high school's only guidance counselor. She had worked there for forty-five years and remembered every student who'd gone to Carlton High during that time.

I walked out to the hallway, then went back into the office, where a young brown-haired secretary was typing at a computer. "There's a man out there with a gun," I said to her.

She looked out the door and giggled. "I know," she said. "The police chief called."

I glanced out at the patrolman. He was close enough to hear everything I said. Unlike the secretary, he did not giggle. "Do you think he'll stop me if I steal the erasers?" I said to the secretary.

"I don't know. You'd better not try it though." She giggled again. She was cute, this giggling secretary. I wondered how she'd look in the future offices of the Scofield Detective Agency in the Empire Building.

I walked out the door again, down a hallway lined with lockers, and into Alice Moyer's office. The office was crammed with file cabinets, bookshelves, a metal desk, and three chairs. The bookshelves held college catalogs, journals and magazines, volumes of studies and statistics, and books on every imaginable occupation. Ms. Moyer was talking to a boy about working as a truck driver. He looked none too bright. I hoped he wouldn't drive down my street.

The boy finally left and Ms. Moyer invited me to sit down across the desk from her. She was close to retirement age, and she looked like the grandmother you either had or wished you had, complete with gray hair, a gentle face, and unlimited patience. "What can I do for you?" she said.

"I'd like to be a bank president," I said, "but I'll settle for auto mechanics."

She didn't giggle, but she did smile. That was my cue to go on. I introduced myself and told her what I was doing. Then I showed her the picture. "He says his name is Max Brady or Max Burns and that he grew up in Carlton. If he really lived here, he would have graduated about thirty years ago. This is a recent photo."

Ms. Moyer studied the photograph awhile, then shook her head. "No," she said. "Even with twenty-five years of aging, I'm sure I've never seen this man before, unless he had plastic surgery." She handed the picture back.

"Plastic surgery? Is that likely?"

"Not in Carlton. All I meant was that I've never seen anyone who looked like the man in the picture."

"What about the name?"

"I've never heard the name Max Brady or Max Burns around here. There was a family named Brady that lived north of town for a while, but they moved away at least twenty years ago. They came here from Missouri and tried farming, but couldn't make a go of it. In any event, they didn't have any kids in high school."

"Did they have any high-school-age kids who didn't go to school?"

"I don't think so. This is a small community. I would have heard about it, even though the family only lived here about a year. They were transients really. You used to see a lot of families like that."

"But not anymore?"

"No. For better or worse, people like that have moved to Chicago or California or anyplace where they can scrape out a living. Nobody moves to a place like Carlton anymore. There's no future here for anyone but retired people. And frankly, that's what I have to tell the kids. All we're doing here is preparing them to leave."

I thanked Ms. Moyer and started to go. A bell rang somewhere and the hallway suddenly filled with loud, energetic teen-agers. "Mind if I wait until it's safe out there?" I said.

"That would be wise," she said. I looked out the door. Down the hallway, the cop had taken refuge against the wall. This was my chance to grab the erasers, but I lacked the guts to go out there with all those kids. I didn't mind taking on Karl Deutsch once in a while, but I knew my limits.

¥

In three minutes, the tumult began to subside. Then the bell rang again. I stuck my head out the door and saw that the danger had passed. The cop was still leaning against the wall. He tried to look relaxed, but I could see that the experience had unnerved him.

I walked back to the superintendent's office and obtained permission to look through old enrollment lists. With the help of Ms. Giggles, I checked the enrollments for all grades in the Carlton School District during the period between thirty and forty years before. I found no one named Burns and only one named Brady. Mary Elizabeth Brady had enrolled in the second grade two decades before. She left school one day in April of that school year and never came back.

¥

I climbed into the Chevy and drove away from the school. All I had learned in Carlton was that Max Brady had never lived there. That wasn't much, but it eliminated one of the many lies I'd heard. If you can disprove enough lies, sometimes the truth will emerge.

The cop followed me to the city limits, then turned back, still as vigilant as ever. You never knew when another stranger might drive into town and talk to a guidance counselor. I stopped for lunch at a crossroads café north of Carlton and arrived back in the Quad Cities in the middle of the afternoon. The sky was an infinite blue over the Mississippi as I crossed the Centennial Bridge. It was mid-September, and the river was still safely in its banks. But who knew for how long? Some forecasters were already predicting a major spring flood.

Chapter Fifteen

I drove to my office, erased the answering machine, and threw away the mail. I was fed up with talking to everyone and getting nowhere. It was time to go high tech.

I looked at my watch. Three-thirty. Vic Domino would be awake by now. I picked up the phone and dialed. "Hello, Vic," I said. "How are things in the digital world?"

"Just fine," he said. "How are things outside?"

"Brisk and sunny."

"What month is it?"

"Still September. You should go out more, Vic. Keeps your pores open."

"Too busy. Don't have time. What can I do for you?"

"I have two credit card numbers. I want to see every transaction for the last two months. Places, dates, times, purchases." I gave him the numbers.

"Piece of cake," he said.

"I knew it would be."

"I'll call you tomorrow."

"Thanks."

Ten minutes later I was sitting in the office, trying to decide what to do next, when the phone rang. "Mike?"

"Yeah."

"This is Carlos." He sounded worried.

"Go on."

"Something's happening to Kathy. Deutsch doesn't let her out of his sight. He takes her everywhere she goes and waits until she's ready to leave."

"What's unusual about that?"

"It's that he stays with her everywhere. Even when she goes home. He stays right there. They've been in her apartment now for hours. It's like he's keeping her prisoner. I'll bet Brady told him to do it."

"Maybe."

"Shouldn't we do something? Try to rescue her or something?"

"Let's not get carried away, Carlos. Before we rescue someone, we'd better make sure she needs to be rescued. For all we know, she may have asked Deutsch to stick around."

"So what do we do? Just sit and wait until someone kills her?"

"No. First, we try not to get hysterical. Then we continue to follow Kathy until we find out what's going on. You're not tired of tailing her, are you?"

"Oh no."

"Didn't think so. I'll relieve you tonight. Okay?"

"Okay, Mike." He hung up.

I went back to my apartment and took it easy the rest of the afternoon. After dinner I drove over to Rock Island and told Carlos to go home. He said he'd be back in an hour, but I told him not to come back until morning. He grumbled about this. I don't think he trusted me to look after Kathy. Finally, he started his car and drove away.

Time passed. It was completely dark out. The temperature dropped, and it got cold in the Chevy. Every now and then I started the engine and ran the heater, just to stay loose in case Deutsch came down to spar a few rounds. His fat-tire car stood at the curb, right in front of the entrance to the Sheridan Apartments, half a block in front of me. He was still upstairs with Kathy, unless he had slid down a drainpipe and swum home. Given the lateness of the hour, it appeared that Kathy would not be appearing at the Gentleman's Retreat tonight.

More time passed. At one-thirty in the morning, a teen-age boy came walking down the sidewalk toward me from the opposite end of the block. Just as he reached Deutsch's car, a Pontiac coming down the street behind him reached the same point. At that moment, guns appeared in both the front and back windows of the Pontiac and let loose with a rapid, deafening series of shots. The kid on the sidewalk fell to the ground, and the car took off with a squeal of rubber on asphalt.

I dropped down to avoid being seen as the car sped by. I didn't want to get into a gunfight with these characters. I always carry my Browning automatic when I'm working, but it's no match for Uzis and AK-47's. As soon as the coast was clear, I sat up and called 911 on my cell phone. Then I got out and ran down the street to Deutsch's car. The kid was lying on the sidewalk with a small hole on one side of his head and a larger hole on the other side. I felt for his pulse. He didn't have one. Childhood was nothing like it used to be.

In the distance, a siren started to wail, followed by another. Much closer, I heard the sound of a car coming rapidly down one of the side streets. I knew who would be in it, and I didn't mean the milkman. I took out my automatic, pulled back and released the slide, and leaned on the trunk of Deutsch's car. The punks came roaring around the corner in their Pontiac, intending to fire another salvo just to make sure the kid was still dead.

I had the element of surprise on my side and I didn't waste it. Before the kid behind the wheel could think of an alternate plan, I shot out his windshield. Everyone in the car ducked. The car swerved wildly. I jumped aside just before it smashed into Deutsch's car at forty or fifty miles an hour.

Suddenly, the street was full of cops. The punks in the back seat jumped out and tried to make a run for it, but two young patrolmen quickly ran them down. The two kids in the front seat weren't in shape for a footrace. Both had ignored the National Safety Council's advice to fasten their seat belts. They were barely conscious and both were bleeding from multiple wounds. I didn't feel sorry for them. They would live. The kid with the hole in his head wouldn't.

An ambulance arrived and two paramedics made a valiant but hopeless effort to revive the kid on the sidewalk. Two more ambulances drove up and the paramedics pulled the bloody-faced killers out of the car and hauled them away.

Detective Lieutenant Brendan Doyle arrived, along with a squad of evidence technicians. They all looked exhausted. You never really get adjusted to being pulled out of bed in the middle of the night.

Doyle was tall and knobby, with hands the size of skillets. His features were hard and angular. No brush or comb had ever mastered his curly brown hair. I told him what had happened. I didn't know why it had happened, but I could guess.

Doyle doesn't usually like to see me on his side of the river, but this time he made an exception. It's hard to find reliable murder witnesses at one-thirty in the morning. Doyle was even kind enough to confirm my suspicions. The punks in the stolen car were members of a drug gang. The kid they had murdered was a drug dealer, although his gang connections were unclear.

Doyle didn't have to tell me the race of each of the five kids. I could see that for myself. The dead kid was white. Two of his killers were white and two were black. In Rock Island, crime was an equal-opportunity employer.

Once Doyle had excused me, I got back into the Chevy and headed home. The police would be working at the crime scene most of the night, and they wouldn't want me in the way. As I drove off, I saw Deutsch standing on the sidewalk, looking sadly at the remains of his car.

Chapter Sixteen

The alarm clock woke me at nine-thirty the morning after the shooting. I ate breakfast at home and picked up a copy of the *Quad-City Times* on the way to the office. The phone was ringing when I got there. I let it ring, sat down, and unfolded the paper.

The murder in Rock Island had made the front page, of course. My own name appeared in the story more times than I thought necessary. A private eye likes to maintain a low profile. Too much publicity scares away clients.

What I found interesting in the story was the career of Richard Miner, the murdered teenager. Only sixteen at the time of his death, he had been one of the Quad Cities' most successful drug dealers. This success had resulted from his ability to provide his customers with a wide variety of drugs, including delicacies such as cocaine, crack, heroin, marijuana, hash, uppers, downers, PCP, and steroids.

Steroids. Until I saw that word right there on page one, I had assumed that the murder of Richard Miner was unrelated to my current investigation. Now I wasn't so sure. Deutsch looked like a steroid user. Maybe he was also a dealer. I wished I could talk to the punks who had killed Miner, but I knew the police wouldn't let me. So I picked up the phone and called Carlos instead. "What's happening over there today?" I said.

"Not much," he said. "Kathy still hasn't come out. I'm worried about her."

"What about Deutsch?"

"Haven't seen him either. The police hauled his car away early this morning. It didn't look so hot with its windows shot out and its side caved in. Do you think we should go in to check on Kathy?"

"No. I think we should wait. What do you know about Richard Miner?"

"He's from Rock Island. That's all I know."

"Why don't you make some calls today while you're waiting for Kathy to beam down."

"Okay." He didn't sound enthusiastic. Little Kathy Dove-Linn absorbed his thoughts.

"Good. Talk to you later."

I hung up, went downstairs, and drove out to the River Village Addition. It looked even more desolate than the last time I'd been there. I didn't see another living soul, not even a cop. The house at 129 Rose Street still stood in a sea of dried mud. A house down the street, the only one occupied in that block during my earlier visit, now stood vacant. Vandals had already broken out most of its windows, and it looked as forlorn as all the houses around it.

I walked around to the rear of 129 Rose and found that someone had broken down the back door since my last visit. I've never been able to resist an unlocked door. I even have trouble resisting locked ones. I walked inside.

The place was still full of mud. The Merry Maids hadn't arrived yet. I poked around for a while, not sure what I was looking for. On a shelf above the kitchen sink, I found a variety of kitchen utensils, including one with a wooden handle. I reached up and grabbed it. It turned out to be the handle of a shiny new Gerhart-Brooks butcher knife. I was relieved to find that it wasn't sticking out of someone's chest.

ᛣ

I couldn't help wondering why the knife was there. Was it just a coincidence, or did a lunatic plan to stick it into someone's chest? If so, who was that lunatic? Max Brady? Karl Deutsch? And who was the intended victim? I hesitated to guess for fear that my own name would come to mind.

I held the knife up to the light from a window and sighted along the blade. No fingerprints. I didn't know what else to do with the knife, so I wiped off my own prints and put it back on the shelf. I looked through the rest of the house, finding nothing else to arouse my interest. Then I drove back to the office. It was almost eleven when I unlocked the door and opened the windows.

The answering machine had taken messages from several reporters, all of whom had questions about the Miner shooting. I erased the tape and walked to the window to stare at the abandoned building across the street. Its vacant eyes stared back, inscrutable as ever.

I paced for a few minutes. Then I sat down and did a little paperwork, although my heart wasn't in it. Finally, I got tired of waiting. I called Vic Domino and was surprised to find him already awake.

"What did you find for me, Vic?" I asked.

"Just what you wanted, Mike."

"Let's have it."

"No activity in the Burns Visa account during the last two months. The Brady Mastercard account was used several times during the same period, mostly for clothes, household items, the usual stuff. Then all in the same day, two and a half weeks ago, Brady ate breakfast at Ruth's Café in Iowa City, stopped for a snack at the North Star Restaurant in Des Moines, and bought gas at Leo's at the Interstate 80 interchange north of Avoca." Avoca was a little burg at the western end of the state.

"A real man of the world," I said.

"I guess so," Vic said.

"Leaves a pretty obvious trail."

"Yeah."

"Maybe too obvious."

"Maybe. You're the detective, Mike. I just find and report."

"Any activity in either account since then?"

"Not a kopeck."

"Keep your eyes on both of them for me, Vic. Run a tab. I'll stay in touch."

"My pleasure."

I pondered Vic's report: Brady appeared to have left town two and a half weeks ago. And the people I had questioned about him claimed not to have seen him since. How convenient. Brady had left town right before Jason King was murdered, which implied that he could not have committed that murder.

I called Carlos again and told him I was going to Iowa City, Des Moines, and Avoca. If he was jealous, he didn't show it. He said that Kathy still hadn't emerged from her tower and that he was still checking on the late Richard Miner.

I went home, packed my bag, and headed west on Interstate 80. My first stop was at Ruth's Café in Iowa City, where I ate lunch and showed everyone my photograph of Max Brady. One of the waitresses remembered him well. He had told her at least three times how excited he was to be moving to Omaha. The waitress hadn't thought it sounded all that exciting herself, but she had humored him and he left a nice tip.

I headed west again on I-80, stopping about two hours later at the North Star Restaurant in Des Moines. I showed the photo of Brady to the cashier, and she remembered him. He had told her, at some length, how happy he was about his move to Omaha. I was beginning to see a pattern.

I reached Leo's Service at the I-80 interchange north of Avoca late in the afternoon. Leo himself told me that Jerry Stonehammer had been on duty the day that Brady bought a tank of gas. Unfortunately, Jerry wasn't there to talk to me right then. He had taken the day off to go hunting. I already had a good idea of what Brady had told him, so I wasn't disappointed.

The disappointment came when I reached Omaha thirty minutes later. Brady's trail, which had been so warm, now turned as cold as an egg in an iceberg. For the rest of the day and most of the next, I talked to all the usual people, and no one had ever seen or heard of Max Brady. Not the police, not the desk clerks or bellboys, not the friendly people at the phone company or the electric company, not the people at the post office or the water department, not even the cab drivers or call girls.

One full day after my arrival, I gave up and headed home, stopping along the way at Leo's Service north of Avoca. I showed the picture of Brady to attendant Jerry Stonehammer and he remembered him immediately. "He wouldn't stop talking about moving to Omaha," he said. "I didn't see what the big deal was myself." Stonehammer had a flat nose and a bushy brown mustache. Chest hairs poked out the top of his T-shirt, which said "Ducks Unlimited" on both the front and back.

"Did he say where he was going to work or live?" I said.

"No, he just kept saying what a great town Omaha was."

"Did he mention any other towns?"

"No, but there was one thing I didn't understand." Stonehammer scratched his neck.

"What was that?"

"When he left here, he drove on up to the interchange."

"Yes?"

"I couldn't understand it."

"What?"

"If he was going to Omaha, why did he turn east in the opposite direction?"

Chapter Seventeen

I climbed into the car, started the engine, and sat there with my brain idling, Stonehammer's question revolving slowly in my thoughts. If Brady was going to Omaha, why did he turn east on I-80, which would take him in the opposite direction? The first town of much consequence in that direction was Des Moines. But if he wanted to go to Des Moines, why did he drive two hundred miles out of his way? Only one good answer to these questions came to mind: He wanted anyone who might be following him to think he was going to Omaha when he was actually going to Des Moines. But did he really go to Des Moines, or was that just another trick? Did he turn east on I-80 because he wanted Stonehammer to see and remember him doing it?

I sat there wondering what to do next. I had been looking forward to going home and sleeping in my own bed. But should I now drive to Des Moines and look all over hell for the slippery Max Brady? Or should I forget the whole thing and drive to Yucatán? Winter was coming. A man had to think about his health.

I took the phone out of my pocket and called Carlos.

"Mike," he said. "I just tried to call you." He sounded agitated.

"I was talking to a guy at a gas station," I said. "What's the trouble?"

"It's Kathy. She's disappeared."

"Did she disappear on purpose, or did someone cause her to disappear?"

"It's Deutsch. I'm sure of it. He picked her up yesterday afternoon. I followed them for a while, but lost them in the traffic on Arsenal Island. I looked everywhere but couldn't find them. Finally, I went back to her building and waited, but she never came back. I waited all night. Then just a few minutes ago, I spotted Deutsch driving an old Ford down West Third Street in Davenport. He was alone. I'll bet he did something to her. She probably found out something about him, and he thought he had to keep her quiet. We have to do something, Mike, right away."

Throughout this rush of words, I kept hoping for a pause where I could insert a calming word or phrase to prevent Carlos from detonating. Finally, I jumped in.

"Carlos," I said.

He kept talking.

"Carlos!" I said.

He paused. "Yeah, Mike?" he said. He was panting.

"Carlos, try to remain calm. If Kathy is in trouble, we have to stay calm in order to help her. I'll be there in four hours or less." I could see that the visit to Des Moines would have to be delayed. "Wait for me. Don't do anything rash. I don't really think either Deutsch or Brady wants to harm Kathy. So wait for me. Understand?"

"Sure, Mike."

"Meet me at the office."

"Okay."

"Don't do anything stupid."

"Okay. Sure. Don't worry."

Don't worry? Fat chance. Young people like Carlos inspire more worry than nuclear weapons, climate change, and bad breath combined. I pulled onto Interstate 80 and outran everything I could in getting back to Davenport. I went straight to the office, where my fears were immediately confirmed. Carlos was as absent as a robin in January. I tried to call him, but got no answer, so I waited.

Half an hour later Carlos still hadn't checked in. I tried to call him again. Still no answer. It wasn't like him to be this late. Now I began to worry. First Kathy had disappeared and now Carlos. Maybe Carlos had been right. Maybe he had confronted Deutsch and gotten his neck broken. He was impulsive enough, especially where Kathy was concerned. I stood up and sprang into action.

Springing into action is tough for me in the best of times. A day on the road had made it even tougher. I would have preferred springing into bed, especially with Carlotta, but that wasn't one of my options for keeping Carlos and Kathy out of harm's way. I locked the office and went down to the car.

I drove the length of West Third and West Fourth Streets a couple of times. I went to the Gentleman's Retreat and looked around. I crossed the river and stared at the Sheridan Apartments for a while. I parked in front of Brady's house, walked across the lawn, and peered in the windows. I went to Carlos's apartment and found no one home. I went everywhere I could think of. Finally, at eleven o'clock that night, I spotted Deutsch going into the Gentleman's Retreat. He was alone. He came out ten minutes later and drove away in a new white Pontiac with conventional tires. I followed along about a block behind.

He drove east on River Drive to Bettendorf, where he took Interstate 74 across the Memorial Bridge to Illinois. After crossing the river, he pulled off the freeway and followed Highway 92 through Moline and East Moline to Silvis. In Silvis, he drove down First Avenue, turned left onto a bumpy dead-end street, and went past a no-trespassing sign. I turned off my lights and followed him. I knew by now where he was going, although I didn't know why.

Deutsch crossed a set of railroad tracks and parked his car in a lot beside the repair shops that had once belonged to the Chicago, Rock Island, and Pacific Railroad, back when the "Rock Island Line" was more than just the title of a folk song. On any business day in the first half of the twentieth century, you would have found hundreds of workers in those shops, repairing the railroad's cars and locomotives. Another company took over the shops after the Rock Island went bankrupt in 1980, and only a small number of people still worked there by the time Deutsch led me down that bumpy street.

I parked my car behind the old administrative building where Deutsch wouldn't see it. Then I crossed the tracks on foot. In the dim light of the moon, I saw Deutsch walking into one of the long brick repair sheds. I followed him in and found myself in almost total darkness. The only light came through the door behind me and the other door at the far end of the shed. I stepped into the darkness on the right side and waited. Ahead of me, Deutsch was standing beside a diesel locomotive. Quietly, almost reverently, he said, "When's the next train?"

I didn't know what response he expected, but it wasn't the one he got. A gun fired, its sound enlarged by reverberation inside the shed. The slug hit the locomotive and ricocheted a couple of times before thudding into a piece of wood somewhere. Deutsch turned and ran like hell for the door. The gunman emerged from his hiding place and started after him.

I had stayed where I was, just inside the door, in the darkness to the right. Deutsch now ran past me like a fat rooster. I wanted Deutsch to stay alive until he led me to Kathy and Carlos, so when the gunman ran past, I stuck my foot out and sent him sprawling. He came to rest face down just inside the doorway. I'm not the quickest person in the world, but when danger is present, I can move pretty fast. Before the gunman could start to get up, I landed on top of him and shoved my automatic into his back.

"Don't move," I said. "Don't even breathe." He didn't move, and for several seconds he took me literally and stopped breathing. I grabbed his revolver, which was still in his hand. "Let go of it," I said. He released his grip, and I slipped the gun into my jacket pocket. "Don't move," I said. Outside, Deutsch's car started with a roar and took off.

I took out my flashlight, turned it on, pointed it at the gunman, and stood up. He was wearing khaki pants, a light-weight jacket, and running shoes. "Okay," I said, "I want you to get up real slow, put your hands up, and turn around." The man got to his feet, raised his hands, turned around, and revealed the embarrassed, youthful face of Carlos Lorca.

Chapter Eighteen

We walked out of the repair shed and stood in the moonlight. To the east, the sheds and sidings lay in the darkness. To the west, the lights of Silvis filled the sky. Somewhere in the distance, a train rumbled along. "Carlos," I said, "I suppose you thought that killing Deutsch would help you find Kathy."

"I wasn't trying to kill him," Carlos said.

"Then why did you shoot at him? Did you think a bullet in the head would improve his memory?"

"I was just trying to scare him."

"Scare him? What for? And why didn't you meet me at the office as you said you would? What's going on in your little brain?"

"I spotted Deutsch right after you called me. I didn't want to lose him, so I couldn't get to the office."

"And?"

"I followed him into a sporting-goods store, then stopped him when he left. I asked him what had happened to Kathy, but he told me to mind my own business. I warned him something would happen to him if he didn't tell me, but he just laughed at me and walked away."

"That was lucky for you. I'm always delighted to see him walking away from me. How did you lure him out here?" I nodded toward the repair shed.

"I followed him to a bar in Davenport. Then I called my brother, and he called Deutsch and pretended to have some steroids for sale."

"Very clever. But if you could call your brother, why couldn't you call me?"

"I tried once, but you didn't answer."

"Which left you free to shoot Deutsch."

"No, I just wanted to scare him."

"Well, Carlos, I think you succeeded. He's so scared that we'll probably never find him again. You didn't think of that, did you?"

There was a lengthy silence, during which he stared at the ground. "No."

"Carlos, I thought you understood this job, but I can see that I was wrong. There are some things a detective never does, and this is one of them. He never shoots just to scare somebody. He doesn't even take the gun out of its holster. The only time you use a gun is to defend yourself or someone else, or to apprehend someone. Only criminals use guns to scare people. When the cops, even private cops, start acting like the robbers, then all you have left is robbers. Do you see what I mean?"

He pushed some gravel around with his foot. "Yes."

"You're lucky as hell you didn't kill him. How would you explain that to anyone? 'Oh, sorry, I just meant to scare him.' Do you think any district attorney in the country would believe that?"

He pushed some more gravel around. "No, Mike."

"You're right. Now let's get the hell out of here before someone finds out who shot his locomotive."

ʃ

I needed a beer and so did Carlos, so we drove to Silvano's Bar in Moline. Silvano's occupied the first floor of an old three-story, red-brick building surrounded by new buildings made of pre-cast concrete. Silvano was still master of his immediate environment. He owned his building. Otherwise, some developer would have already reduced it to red dust and recollections. I prefer a real bar to a recollection any day. I can always recollect the taste of Beck's Dark, but I need occasional real-time transfusions to keep the memory vivid.

Carlos and I found a table and sat down. The place consisted of a large room with a bar along one wall and tables scattered about elsewhere. A back-bar with a perfectly preserved mirror covered the wall behind the bar. Black and white photographs of log rafts, sawmills, and factories hung on the wall opposite the bar. The men in the photographs were wearing work clothes and heavy boots. I looked around the room. No one at Silvano's was wearing work clothes and heavy boots that evening, myself included. We couldn't have turned logs into two-by-fours if we had to.

I looked away from the photographs and ordered beers for Carlos and me. After taking my first drink, I set the glass down and looked at Carlos. "Carlos," I said, "I know you had a lot on your mind while I was gone, but I wonder if you had time to ask any questions about the late Richard Miner, teenage drug king of Rock Island. Forgot about it, didn't you?"

"No, I didn't forget about it," he said with resentment. He was tired of my criticism. "I did it before Kathy disappeared." He took a drink.

"Sorry. Forgive me for doubting you."

"That's all right." The defensive tone went out of his voice.

"What did you find out?"

"I saw in the paper that Miner had graduated from Rock Island High School, so I went to the public library and looked up the yearbook. I photocopied the names of all the kids in his class and started calling them."

"Excellent, Carlos, excellent."

Carlos grinned at this praise. He had already forgotten the unpleasantness at the repair shops. "It didn't take long to find out something about him," he said. "Now that he's dead, plenty of kids were willing to talk about him."

"That always makes a difference," I said.

"Everybody knew that Miner was dealing dope, but no one knew where he was getting it."

"Go on."

"A few kids saw him with an older guy now and then. The guy sometimes gave him a ride."

"Yes."

"They didn't know his name, but when I asked them what he looked like, the man they described sounded like Max Brady."

"Ahhh." I sat back in the chair and took another drink. Max Brady. Everywhere I went I met Max Brady coming back. Figuratively, that is. I would have paid plenty to meet him in real life. Or rather, Morrison would have paid plenty.

"No one knew for sure who Brady was or why Miner would be hanging around with him," Carlos said.

"But we have a good idea, don't we? Miner was a drug dealer, and my guess is that Brady was one of his suppliers. With all his other shady business activities, Brady would have the connections. We already know that the punks who killed Miner were members of a drug gang that didn't want his competition. The night he was killed, Miner was probably going to the Sheridan Apartments to meet Deutsch. It all makes sense."

"What does all this have to do with Jason King's murder?" Carlos said.

"That's a question I'd like to ask Max Brady, if he's still anywhere in this galaxy. I'd like to find Deutsch and ask him, too, but I don't think he enjoys my company."

"Probably not."

"Someone was stealing drugs from the downtown Morco. Brady could have been involved in that, although he'd need plenty of other sources for cocaine and other delecasies. Maybe King was involved in all this and got himself killed."

"By Brady or Deutsch," Carlos said.

"Right," I said.

"And then one of them killed Meiers because he knew too much about the flood-relief scam and the drugs."

"Right again."

"But why did the one who did it kill them both with the same kind of butcher knife?"

I hesitated a moment. "I don't know," I said, "unless he's crazy."

"Or maybe Brady and Deutsch want everyone to think the killer is crazy," he said. "Maybe they think that will throw everybody off their trail."

"Maybe." We both fell silent for a while, sipping our beers and letting our brilliant minds sort, file, and retrieve. "Did you find out anything else about Miner?" I finally asked.

"No, that's it."

We had reached the limits of our knowledge, so we let the subject rest. Carlos went to call his brother, and I noticed that our glasses were empty. I ordered another round, then looked at one of the old photos on the wall. A factory worker with a thick, dark mustache was staring at me from the middle of the nineteenth century. His body was lean and strong. His black eyes revealed no doubts or uncertainties. For a moment I had the sensation that he was asking me just what the hell we had done to his town.

Chapter Nineteen

The next morning, I decided to report to the boss before continuing my search for Max Brady. Morrison was as tight as the skin on a green banana, and I had learned to keep him informed about how I was spending his money. After opening the mail and listening to the answering machine, I walked from my office to Morrison's. The weather was cool and partly cloudy. I was dressed for the season in a tweed jacket, blue shirt, and red tie, all of which I had bought at Penney's. I could afford better clothes, but I didn't want Morrison to know it. He might decide he was paying me too much.

As usual I arrived thirty minutes late, but Morrison was onto my game and kept me waiting another ten. I passed the time joking with Barbara Faber, his secretary. She knew I was harmless, so she humored me. Morrison finally buzzed her, and she let me into the throne room.

The great man's office was still as big as ever. His mahogany desk gleamed the gleam of the rich and powerful. Through the broad window behind him, I saw a towboat pushing six barges of grain downriver. Morrison had a terrific view. I wondered if he ever turned around and looked out.

I sat down and tried to look at Morrison instead of the river. It was hard to do. The river was far more interesting. "I wanted to let you know how the investigation of Jason King's murder was going," I said. I had decided not to bother him with how my affair with his wife was going.

"Good," he said. "What have you learned?" He attempted to look interested, but I knew he'd rather be negotiating a toilet-paper contract.

"First of all, I learned that someone has been stealing drugs from the downtown Morco. At least two people think King was responsible. I assume you were aware of this problem."

His face reddened slightly. "Yes, I knew about it. Jason was trying to solve the matter. I think he suspected one of the pharmacists."

"Did he say which one?"

"No, he wanted to talk to all of them first."

"Did you notify the police?"

"Well, no, I didn't want to make an issue of it until I knew all the facts. An incident like that can give the public a bad impression."

"An incident like that can land you in prison."

He reflected on this. "You're right," he said. "I'll call Chief Mittendorf. Just leave it to me."

I stared at him. I had my doubts, but he was the boss. "All right," I said.

"What else did you find out?" he said. He wanted to get me off the topic of the stolen drugs. I let him do it.

"I located a young woman who was in the store the night of the murder," I said. "With what I learned from her, I found several people who might've been involved, although their exact relationships to each other aren't entirely clear."

"So you don't really know who might have done it." He tapped the desk top with his index finger.

"Not yet, but I'm getting closer. I need more time."

"And what do you expect to find out?"

"What I've learned so far points to the involvement of a man named Max Brady. I need to talk to him, but I haven't caught up with him yet. He's been involved in a variety of shady deals, including possible drug operations. Almost everyone seems to know him. I think he might be the key to the whole thing."

"Max Brady?"

"That's right. Do you know him?"

"I know who he is, although I've never met him. He owns a lot of run-down properties around town."

"That's right," I said, "and I think he used some of those properties to defraud the government after the flood last spring. That's one of the things I want to ask him about."

"He defrauded the government?" Morrison said as he leaned forward and stared at me.

"That's how it looks. He recruited some winos on West Third Street to file bogus claims for flood damages. They all reported that they lived in the houses he owned in the River Village

Addition, and they claimed losses on furniture and other personal property. Then he turned around and sold those same houses to something called River Village Enterprises. When I tried to find out who owned that company, I got nowhere at all."

Morrison continued to stare at me. I thought he was going to say something, but he didn't. "I thought maybe Brady was trying to hide his ownership of those properties by selling them to himself," I said. Morrison seemed interested, so I stuck with that theme. "Do you have any idea who owns River Village Enterprises?"

He hesitated. "Yes, I know who owns it," he said.

"That's great," I said. "Who?"

He sat back in his leather chair. His eyes never left my face. "I do," he said.

☧

I don't know how long I sat there with my mouth open, but a dentist could have filled at least one cavity and maybe more. Finally, I said, "You own it?"

"Yes," he said.

"I thought you said you never met Max Brady."

"I never met him face to face. Someone else did that for me. Brady gave me a good price, and I took advantage of it."

"May I ask what you're going to do with all those worthless houses?"

He hesitated, then leaned forward and clasped his hands. "I assume that this information will remain confidential, as with all business matters that you and I discuss."

"Of course."

He leaned back and smiled. "I'm going to tear them down and build a shopping mall."

"And you don't want the competition to know about it in advance." I said this merely to show him that I understand how big business operates.

"Exactly. I want to keep it quiet until the last possible moment."

"You must be planning something big."

"Big enough. The building and parking lot will cover the eight square blocks at the south end of the River Village Addition. I'm going to call it the River Village Shopping Mall. There's nothing like it in the West End. I see it as a major new service for the people down there."

I always felt a little sick at my stomach when Morrison started using the word "service" in connection with his business operations, as if he were bathing lepers or feeding orphans, all at no charge. I didn't say that, though. I said, "With a Morco Drugstore?"

"Certainly," he said. "The people of the West End deserve one as much as anyone else." That about said it all. Saint William had arrived in the West End.

"I couldn't agree more," I said, the lie whistling through my teeth. "Now that you've let me in on your plans, could you induce George Mann to help me find Max Brady. He wouldn't tell me a thing when I talked to him."

"Sure. Of course. I'll be happy to talk to him. Now that you know about everything, there's no need for secrecy."

Morrison had become downright convivial. I'd never seen him so cheerful. "Could you call him right away?" I said. "This morning?"

"I'll be happy to. You understand, of course, that George was simply looking after my best interests when he wouldn't answer your questions. He's an excellent property manager, and also an old friend of mine."

"I understand. I have one other question, though."

"Yes?" His tone suggested that in spite of his good mood, he was getting tired of my questions and I should start looking for the door.

"How are you going to keep the water out of your shopping mall every time the river floods? It does that a lot down there, you know."

"Dikes. We'll build dikes on three sides. The side farthest from the river is already high enough that it doesn't flood." He smiled proudly, happy to have thought of everything. Then he stood up to say goodbye. I got the hint and did the same. At that moment, the sun came from behind a cloud, and light streamed through the window behind him, creating a perfect halo around Morrison's head.

༄

I stopped for a cup of coffee at Vigo's Café before going to see George Mann. One cup led to two more. Finally, I said so long to Vigo and walked outside. The day was still cool. I shoved my hands into my pockets and walked to the Empire Building.

The elevator took me to the tenth floor, where I strolled down the hall to the offices of George Mann and the Property Management Associates. I walked in with neither a knock nor an appointment, but this time they knew I was coming. The secretary was almost friendly.

She motioned me to a chair and I watched as she spoke to Mann on the phone, which hardly seemed necessary, given that he was only ten or twelve feet away. It occurred to me how strange it was that modern communications devices actually kept people apart. I thought about writing a treatise on this idea, but I didn't think the *Private Investigator's Journal* or *Security Today* would buy it.

The secretary had on the same pearls she had worn during my first visit, but she was wearing a different dress. This one was blue and sleek with a low-cut neckline. Her hair was still dark, her eyes still blue. I was about to ask her to marry me, when George Mann suddenly came out of his office all smiles and affability. He still had the same brown hair and pinstripe suit.

"Mike," he said, shaking my hand vigorously. "Good to see you again." He put a brotherly hand on my shoulder and ushered me into his office. He sat down at his desk, and I sat down across from him, which gave neither of us much to look at.

"Mike," Mann said, "I wish you'd told me the other day you worked for William Morrison."

"So do I."

"I would've told you anything you wanted to know. Bill Morrison is an old friend and a valued customer. There's nothing I wouldn't do for him."

"That's good to hear. I need—"

"How is he? I haven't seen him for a while. Talk to him on the phone, of course, almost every week."

"He's fine, just fine. And if he does get sick, he'll have all the drugs he needs."

Mann missed this witticism. "You bet he will," he said. "You bet he will. Now what can I help you with today?" He folded his hands in his lap and looked at me with all the warmth he could generate.

"I'm still looking for Max Brady," I said. "I was hoping you could help me find him."

"Yes, I remember you were interested in Max Brady. I'm afraid, though, that I have no idea where he is." He smiled cheerfully, happy to share his ignorance of Brady's whereabouts.

"He's quite the real-estate operator, in spite of his constant absence. Did you know that he owns both the Marquette Hotel and the Gentleman's Retreat?"

"No, I wasn't aware of that, but it doesn't surprise me. He has a reputation for buying run-down properties as cheaply as possible in hopes of reselling them and making an easy profit."

"Just as he did with all those houses in the River Village Addition," I said.

"Exactly," he said, poking the air with his right forefinger, "but keep in mind that he asked a reasonable price. He never damages his own chance of success by setting his prices unrealistically high. He's very shrewd and not a bit greedy. He'll settle for a sure fifty thousand any day, rather than hold out for fifty-five and lose a sale altogether."

"Sounds like quite a guy. I'd like to meet him. Did he ever tell you what his hometown was? He's apparently not from around here."

"Let me think." Mann screwed up his face in concentration. "I think he once said he was from Carlton." He pondered this a moment. "Yes, that's it. That's what he said, Carlton, Illinois. I can't swear he was telling the truth, but you could drive down and check it out."

Sure, I thought, I could drive off a cliff, too. I didn't want to spoil his moment of sharing by telling him I'd already wasted enough time in Carlton, so I thanked him for his help and made my exit. The secretary was nowhere in sight when I walked out, so I had to delay my marriage proposal again. The course of true love ran no more smoothly than the Mississippi in March or April.

※

Both George Mann and Fred Hutz, the desk clerk at the Marquette Hotel, had given me the same incorrect information about Brady's hometown. Brady was apparently a consistent liar. He didn't name a different town every time someone asked him the same question. He was honest enough to tell the same lie to two different people.

I walked from the Empire Building to my office at Fourth and Brady, where I let myself in, sat down, and picked up the phone book. I don't often call police agencies for information. It's usually a waste of time. Cops don't like to give information to private detectives. They want you to give information to them. This may not seem equitable, but that's the way it is.

In spite of this, I sometimes have to face the humiliation of calling the cops. I looked up a Davenport number and dialed. A man answered. "FBI," he said. I could tell from his tone that he usually didn't have to answer the telephone and that he didn't like doing it.

"I want to report some fraudulent claims for emergency flood relief," I said.

The man didn't reply. He just moved the phone away from his mouth and shouted, "Riley, phone on line three."

I looked out the window as I waited for Riley. I had a clear view of the Federal Building, which is where Riley was. If he looked out his window, we could wave. The phone clicked a couple of times and a voice said, "Mark Riley speaking. What can I do for you?" He spoke with a tired voice that suggested he really didn't want to do anything for me. I acted as if I hadn't noticed.

"This is Michael Scofield," I said. "I'm a private investigator. I'm conducting an investigation for a client, and I've come across some information about fraudulent claims for federal flood relief."

"Who's the client?"

"Sorry, I can't say."

"Is the client involved in the fraud?"

"I don't think so," I said. "He has so much money already that he can't stuff anymore into his mattress. He's past the fraud stage."

"How nice for him," Riley said. "What's the nature of the fraud?" He was talking with more energy now. I'd found a topic that caught his interest.

"A man recruited a crew of alcoholics to file phony flood claims with FEMA."

"What part of town?"

"The River Village Addition."

"Did this man own the houses where the claimants said they lived?"

"That's right. Most were empty, but he brought some junk in to make them look inhabited."

"What's the man's name?" Riley said.

"Max Brady," I said.

"Just what I expected."

"So this is old news to you."

"Yes, but don't let that discourage you. What else do you have on him?"

"He owns the Marquette Hotel, a flop house for alcoholics. And I suspect he's involved in illegal drug operations. You probably knew all this already."

"Probably."

"You don't know where he is, do you?" I asked. This was the real purpose of my phone call. I didn't want to waste any more time looking for Brady if the feds would tell me where he was.

"Sorry," Riley said. "That's the one thing I don't know about him. I was hoping you could tell me."

"No, I don't know either, but if I find him I'll call you right away. Could you do the same?"

"Oh, sure, sure. I'll call you first thing." He was lying like a door-to-door Bible salesman, but so was I. "I know where his house is here in town. Nice little place up on Clay Street. I got a search warrant to go in and turn the place inside out, but someone beat me to it."

"Oh?"

"Yeah. Someone broke in through the back door and made a mess of the place. You wouldn't know anything about that, would you?"

"Not me, Riley. I can't stand clutter."

"Glad to hear it. I wouldn't want you involved in something like that."

"Couldn't agree more. You might want to keep your eyes open for a thug named Karl Deutsch, though. I'm sure he knows where Brady is, but he isn't telling."

"What's he look like?"

"Short blond hair. About five ten. Steroid head. Slow and stupid, but watch out for him. If he gets close enough to hit you, you'll forget the names of all fifty states."

"Thanks for the warning. If I see him, I'll talk through a bullhorn. Where's he live?"

"Don't know. He's not in the phone book or city directory. He spends a lot of time in his car."

"Does he have a job?"

"Used to be a bouncer at the Gentleman's Retreat. Haven't seen him there recently, though. By the way, Brady owns that dump, too."

"I know," Riley said.

"You know a lot, don't you?" I said.

"I guess so. You have any more information for me?"

"Don't think so."

"If you find Brady, let me know. Understand?"

"Perfectly. One other thing."

"What's that?"

"If you find Deutsch, don't mention his IQ. It makes him grumpy."

Chapter Twenty

I went home for a long lunch. I had to kill time while waiting for a reasonable hour to call Vic Domino. After lunch, I stood with a cup of coffee, looking across Fifth Street at the elevated tracks of the long-dead Chicago, Rock Island, and Pacific Railroad.

While I was still standing there, a diesel locomotive came slowly down the tracks, pulling a string of grain cars. The Iowa Interstate Railroad now owns this stretch of track. The train drew even with my window and rolled on past, which I took as my cue to call Vic Domino. Vic's business provided valuable services, but had a number of faults. These included secrecy, inconvenient hours, and Vic's refusal to come out of his house, wherever that house was.

Someday I planned to have my own computer, hard drive, printer, modem, databases, and associated firepower; along with a gorgeous secretary, several detectives, and a suite of offices in the Empire Building. Actually, I could live without most of that. What I really wanted was the secretary. I picked up the phone and dialed.

"Vic," I said. "It's two o'clock on Friday afternoon. Wake up and smell the packing plant."

"I am awake, and I can't smell it."

"Why not? You a vegetarian?"

"The windows are closed."

"I'm glad to hear you have windows. They're not boarded up, are they?"

"No."

"Bricked up?"

"No, they're not bricked up either, Mike. What do you need today?"

"You were going to continue keeping track of those two credit card numbers for me. Anything happening?"

"Just a sec. . . . Here we go. Nothing until yesterday. Then Max Burns emerged from the primordial slime and bought a tank of gas and some groceries."

"Where did this economic boomlet occur, Vic? Des Moines?"

"No, not Des Moines." There was a pause. "Sabula."

"Sabula?"

"That's right."

"Sabula?"

"You're repeating yourself, Mike."

"Sorry. It's just hard to believe."

"Many things are, Mike."

"I know. . . . You still have the same bank account?"

"You guessed it."

"Send me a bill."

"Will do."

"Thanks, Vic. You're a pal. Keep your eye on him."

"You bet."

He hung up, and so did I. I went back to the window to stare at the track and plan the rest of my day. After a few minutes, I charged into action. I called Carlos. I opened a bottle of Beck's Dark. Then I called Morrison's wife.

Carlotta lay beside me in the darkness. Naked. I couldn't see her, but that didn't matter. I had her memorized. Like a vanished railroad still remembered. The rise and fall of her breasts. The curve of her legs. The sweep of her arms. The turn of her lips. The angle of her nose. The crest of her forehead. Her red hair leaving a trail of sparks in the night.

"Mike?"

"Yes?"

"What are you thinking about?"

"Railroads."

"Do you like railroads?"

"Yes. But I try not to like them too much."

"Why not?"

"They might disappear."

I ran my hand across her stomach and over her breasts. I kissed her throat and her cheek. Then I lay back on the bed. "Across the Des Moines River from the little town of Eldon, Iowa, there used to be a big freight yard. When I was a little boy, we went through there two or three times a year on the way to Kansas City to visit my aunt and uncle. The yard had a roundhouse, a tower, miles of track, switch engines rumbling back and forth, and hundreds of boxcars.

"At the west end, the track led off through the hills. At the other end, the track crossed the river to Eldon on a high steel bridge supported by concrete piers. That freight yard was one of the busiest places in the state. But if you went there today, all you would find is the concrete piers, minus the bridge. Everything else is gone, vanished like a meadowlark in November. Where the tracks used to be, there's nothing but a soybean field. It's as if that freight yard never existed, but I saw it dozens of times. It was more real than the Matterhorn, and now it's gone."

"I know what you mean," she said, and I think she did. Carlotta is like that.

Chapter Twenty-One

Sabula lies fifty miles north of the Quad Cities. Local promoters like to point out that it's the only town in Iowa located on an island. This claim is entirely true, but don't confuse Sabula with Jamaica. Sabula sits in the Mississippi, not the Caribbean. Its shores are made of mud, not sand. And its reggae is nonexistent.

Sabula differs from Jamaica in two additional ways. Jamaica has four thousand square miles. Sabula has thirty square blocks. Jamaica has a population of three million. Sabula has a population of six hundred. Taking everything into consideration, I'd rather search for someone in Sabula than in Jamaica. The odds would be better, although the weather would probably be worse.

The next Monday, at nine o'clock in the morning, I turned onto Highway 64 and drove east across the mile-long causeway to Sabula. Halfway there, a small island held a picnic table and two toilets, just in case you got hungry or your bladder failed during the crossing. Two middle-aged men were fishing off the east side of the island. Neither looked like Max Brady, so I kept going.

The highway reached Sabula at the northern end of the town, crossed the island, and continued on down another causeway toward the high cantilever bridge that spanned the river to Savanna, Illinois. At the southern tip of the island, a set of railroad tracks traversed the town and crossed the river on an ancient steel-truss bridge. The bridge included a long swingspan to accommodate towboats and barges.

I arrived in Sabula and turned south onto a residential street. I drove to the south end of the island and came back on a parallel street. Max Brady didn't rush out to flag me down.

I stopped at the police station to introduce myself. The man on duty didn't recognize Max Brady when I showed him the photograph. I drove around awhile longer, past a gas station, a grocery store, a bar, a post office, a library, a school, a church, a small factory, and several blocks of houses. The island tilted down gently from east to west, as if trying to slide all these buildings off its back. Along the shore on the east side, several middle-aged men were fishing, which seemed to be the primary form of entertainment in Sabula.

I finally parked the car where I could see the grocery store and the bar, both of which stood between the street and the river. Unless Brady had joined AA and gone on a starvation diet, the chances were good that he would eventually make an appearance. I got out my binoculars, the photo of Brady, and my thermos of coffee. I had two potential enemies at this point. One was boredom and the other was the bar across the street. Each in its own way would tempt me to forget where I was and what I was doing.

I taped the photograph to the dashboard. Then I propped the latest *Quad-City Times* on the steering wheel in front of me and pretended to read. Every now and then I turned the page, just so I wouldn't look like a wax dummy.

The wheels of commerce in Sabula turned steadily, though never fast, all morning long. People wandered into the grocery store and wandered back out. Several fishermen abandoned the riverbank and withdrew to the bar to restore the tissues. Down the street behind me, cars and pickups gassed up at the filling station.

On two occasions I temporarily left my post unmanned, once to buy food at the grocery store and once to visit the gents' room at the gas station. At two o'clock in the afternoon, a man came out a side door of an apartment building half a block in front of me and walked across the street toward the bar. He was the first muscle builder I'd ever seen in Sabula. Warning lights began to flash in my brain.

Peering casually over the top of the comics page, I watched the guy cross the street. He was big and tall, and his muscles rippled like an old glass Coke bottle. He had short brown hair, a long face, and a jaw that jutted like a snowplow. His eyes were so close together they almost pushed the nose off his face.

Jutjaw walked into the bar and came out a few minutes later with a twelve-pack of Budweiser. He was wearing a skin-tight polo shirt with horizontal red and white stripes, a pair of tan pants, and shiny brown shoes. He walked back to the apartment house, which was a two-story brick rectangle with a screened porch overlooking the street and, beyond that, the river. The building dated from about 1900. It was attractive but not elegant.

Jutjaw headed toward the side door from which he had emerged, and I focused the binoculars. He opened the door and stepped inside. Before the door closed behind him, I saw another man in the apartment, a man who looked exactly like the one in the photo on my dashboard.

For a second or two, I thought about walking over to the door and barging in, but I didn't want to spend the rest of the year in traction. Jutjaw was no mere strip-joint bouncer like Karl Deutsch. He was bigger in every observable way. He looked as stupid as a mudfish, but that wouldn't matter. It would only make him fearless.

In a violent confrontation with Jutjaw, my only option would be to shoot him, not between the eyes, of course, but somewhere. But if I did, the Iowa Department of Public Safety would start having second thoughts about my detective's license. I'd also have to explain myself to Carlos, no small task after my recent lecture about guns and shooting.

So I stayed in the car and waited for someone to come out. No one did. At ten o'clock that night, I called Davenport. "Carlos," I said, "I'm sitting here in a fisherman's paradise. What's happening there?"

"Karl Deutsch is in the hospital," Carlos said. He sounded agitated, though he tried to hide it.

"Oh, really? What's wrong? Tummy ache?"

"I don't know. No one will say. I guess he's in pretty bad shape."

"You didn't shoot him, did you?" I said.

"Of course not," he said.

"How'd you find out about him?"

"I called the Gentleman's Retreat and asked for him. They said he was in St. Luke's."

"Good work. Stay on top of it."

"What about Brady?"

"He's here in Sabula with another muscle builder."

"What are you gonna do?"

"Stay out of hitting and kicking range. I'll have to wait until I can get to Brady without taking on his friend."

"Mike."

"Yes."

"I still haven't found Kathy. What if Deutsch did something to her? Should I try to question him at the hospital?" His voice grew hoarse with emotion.

"You can try, Carlos, but they probably won't let you near him. Also, try to remember that in the past Deutsch has appeared to be her protector. We have no reason to believe that he'd harm her."

"I know, but I'm worried."

"You worry a lot, Carlos. You'd make a good mother. Maybe you should settle down and raise a family."

"I just don't want anything to happen to her."

"I know. Keep your eyes open. I'll call you tomorrow."

"Okay."

"So long."

I hung up and turned my attention back to Brady's apartment. The lights were on. Brady and Jutjaw were probably reading Spinoza or listening to Verdi. Or both.

At eleven o'clock I made myself a peanut butter sandwich. The car was a mess, with crumbs, food wrappers, and pop cans all over hell. Still no beer bottles, though. At twelve o'clock the lights went off in the apartment. I kept my eyes on the door, but no one came out. Half an hour later, I pushed all the junk onto the floor, lay down on the seat, and went to sleep.

‡

The rumble of car and pickup engines awoke me at dawn. The fishermen were arriving to renew their battle with the catfish. At seven o'clock I went to the gas station to relieve myself. Then I went to the grocery story to buy more stuff to litter the car with, after which I went to the bar for coffee. Back in the car, I removed the lid from the paper cup and took a sip. The coffee tasted like muddy water, so I poured out a third of it and refilled the cup with milk. I took another sip. Now it tasted like muddy milk, which was a definite improvement.

By eight o'clock I was beginning to have questions about my career path. My head hurt and so did my back. My utility flask, lurking in the glove compartment, posed a constant temptation. My condition was becoming critical. Perhaps a less stressful job would help. Something like an air-traffic controller or brain surgeon.

At a quarter till nine I was considering a phone call to my old high school guidance counselor when Brady and Jutjaw suddenly emerged from their bunker and climbed into a dark-blue Pontiac. Brady had on a tan suit, a pale-yellow tie, and dark glasses. Jutjaw was still wearing his muscle-boy outfit. They moved quickly. Jutjaw started the engine and pulled away from the curb. I couldn't tell for sure, but I didn't think they had fastened their seat belts. Two murders, disaster fraud, drug dealing, and now a seat-belt violation: Brady had a lot of explaining to do.

I gave them a head start, then followed along about two blocks behind. They drove to the north end of the island and turned onto Highway 64 toward Savanna. The highway headed north for about two miles along a causeway through the backwater. As I trailed the Pontiac, I looked across the water at Savanna, sitting serenely at the base of its limestone bluff, its hardwood trees in their fall colors standing out against the bluff and the blue sky. Finally, the road turned east and rose from the causeway to the bridge that crossed into Illinois.

I drove across the bridge, turned right onto Main Street, and followed the Pontiac into Savanna's business district. The town still looked prosperous, despite cutbacks at the Savanna Army Depot. Jutjaw drove slowly down the street, finally stopping in front of an old two-story brick storefront. The second floor had three tall, narrow windows crowned with round arches. A modest cornice stood at the top of the wall. Brady climbed out of the car and walked inside. Jutjaw drove on down the street and turned a corner.

I found a place to park a few doors beyond the building. After shutting off the engine, I waited a few minutes before getting out. Jutjaw didn't return, so I walked back down the sidewalk to the building, which I now saw contained the office of James P. White, Doctor of Chiropractic Medicine. Brady apparently had a backache, or something. I saw my chance.

I walked inside and headed for the desk at the far end of the waiting room, where a chunky brown-haired woman in a white uniform was writing something on a desk calendar. She looked up at me with a noncommittal expression and said, "Good morning."

"Hello," I said. "I'm David Long. I need to see Dr. White." I was bending over slightly, as if unable to bear the pain of standing up straight.

"Do you have an appointment?"

"No, but I was hoping to get in to see him anyway. I just hurt my back helping my grandfather get out of bed, and it hurts something awful. Do you think you could possibly squeeze me in?"

I glanced around the waiting room, which was entirely empty except for the woman and me. "Dr. White is with another patient," she said, "but if you'd like to have a seat, I'll try to get you in."

"Thank you. Thank you very much." I turned and walked across the dark-red carpet to one of the gray chairs, where I sat down and fought the pain. The woman paid no attention to this performance, so I picked up a magazine and flipped through it. The queen's family was still wallowing in adultery. A TV actress had a new boyfriend. A basketball star was selling shoes.

It didn't take long to extract all the pleasure you can get from royalty, TV stars, and athletes. Finally, a woman emerged from a hallway at the back of the room and stopped to confer with the woman at the desk. Money changed hands. Both said goodbye, and the patient departed.

The woman at the desk put the money away and shuffled some file folders. Then she looked at me and stood up. "Follow me, please," she said.

I got up and hobbled along behind her as best I could, keeping my eyes open for Brady. My plan was to ask him some pointed questions about drugs, murder, and real estate, if I could corner him before Jutjaw made an appearance. Failing that, I would question Dr. White about Brady. Then I'd return to Brady's apartment in Sabula to wait for his next move.

The woman in the white uniform led me into an examination room, gave me a hospital gown to put on, and walked out, closing the door behind her. After her footsteps had receded, I stepped over to the door and opened it just far enough to see anyone who walked down the hall. Then I hung the gown on a hook and sat down to wait.

Thirty minutes later, I was still waiting. Brady's backache was apparently worse than mine. Finally, a door opened down the hallway, and someone walked toward the waiting room. I stared at the door, expecting to see Brady, but saw a middle-aged woman instead. Rats. This meant that Brady was still in another examination room, waiting to see Dr. White. This could take forever. Or longer.

I sat back down in the chair and prepared for another wait. My stomach was growling. My clothes were rumpled. I needed a shave. I needed coffee. Small wonder that the receptionist hadn't greeted me with much warmth. I was a mess.

I was wondering how much longer I could live without coffee when the door suddenly opened and a man in a white coat entered the room, smiled, and reached out to shake hands. "Good morning, Mr. Long," he said. "I'm Dr. White. What can I do for you today?"

His entrance had come so quickly that I wasn't primed to respond. Instinctively, I stood up and shook hands. He stood there waiting for me to say something, and finally I did. "Good morning," I said. "Good morning, Mr. Brady."

Chapter Twenty-Two

"You must have me confused with someone else," the man said. "My name is White, Doctor James White, not Brady." His tone was still polite, but cautious.

"I'm not confused," I said, "although I can see why you might prefer being known as Dr. White instead of Max Brady. For one thing, the FBI is looking for Brady. On the other hand, from the looks of your waiting room, hardly anyone is looking for Dr. White. Maybe that's why you became Max Brady. Maybe Dr. White wasn't doing so well. Not enough spines to pop in Savanna, perhaps."

"I don't know what you're talking about. You'd better go." He held the door open for me. I didn't use it.

"Don't rush me," I said. "My back is out of joint and information is the only thing that will fix it. To start with, who killed Jason King? I think you know who. In fact, I think you may have done it yourself."

"I don't know anyone by that name. Get out!" He gestured toward the door.

"Or maybe you had someone kill him for you, someone like Karl Deutsch."

"I don't know anyone by that name either."

"Deutsch is in the hospital, by the way. Not doing too well from what I hear. I hope that doesn't make you sad."

For just an instant, I thought I saw a hint of sadness in Brady-White's eyes, but it immediately disappeared. "I don't know him, so why would I be sad?" he said.

"You know," I said, "if you're going to be difficult about this, I think I'll just turn you over to the FBI. They have evidence that you defrauded FEMA and killed Joseph Meiers to cover it up. They'd love to know where you are. I'll have to give them a ring."

"Give them anything you want. I haven't done a thing, and no one can prove that I have." He crossed his arms and assumed a stolid expression.

This line of attack wasn't getting me very far. He was bluffing, but so was I. "All right," I said, "if you're innocent, why don't you tell me who's guilty? If you cooperate with me, I'll forget about FEMA and the FBI. They'll never know I found you."

"You didn't find me. I'm not the man you're looking for."

There was a contradiction somewhere in that statement, but I didn't have time to sort it out. "Then there's the problem of Richard Miner, the murdered drug dealer," I said. "I have witnesses who saw you with him on many occasions. I can put together a good case that you were supplying him with drugs."

"Never heard of him."

"Okay, I've had it. I tried to give you a break, but what good did it do me? None, that's what. You're in trouble, Doctor, big trouble." I started for the door, and that's when I saw that *I* was in big trouble. Jutjaw was standing in the doorway, blocking my exit. This worried me, and not just because it created a fire hazard. The hazard was of a different sort, and it included the likelihood of broken bones and lacerations. My bones, my lacerations.

I thought of a couple of smart remarks, but for once my hand was quicker than my mouth. I retrieved my Browning automatic from my shoulder holster and flicked off the safety. The gun was already cocked, with a 9mm cartridge poised in the chamber. I was through playing punching bag for every moron who could swallow a steroid tablet. "Jutjaw," I said, "get your stupid ass out of the way."

He didn't move. He didn't even flinch. In fact, he looked as if he was about to come over and bend my automatic into a bobby pin. I saw no way to negotiate. There was only one door out of that room, and my appointment was over. I aimed at Jutjaw and shot off his ear lobe.

)(

Suddenly, the balance of power shifted. Jutjaw grabbed his ear, backed out the door, and disappeared down the hallway toward the rear of the building. Dr. Brady-White cringed in a corner. I stepped through the door and ran toward the front, past the startled woman in the white dress and through the empty waiting room.

I stuck my head out the front door and looked around. No Jutjaw. I holstered the automatic, trotted to the car, and jumped in. My ears were still ringing and my hands were still shaking. I didn't know what to do next. I was pretty sure that the next time I saw Jutjaw, he'd be armed with more than just his good looks. With that in mind, should I continue to chase him and Brady-White, or should they chase me? Role definition was becoming complicated.

Fortunately, I had come prepared for problems like this one. I extracted my utility flask from the glove compartment and had a stiff drink. Then I had one more and the truths of the universe suddenly revealed themselves.

Another confrontation with Brady-White and his muscle boy would bring me no closer to solving the case, so I turned instead to Police Chief Walter Metcalf, who had once helped me run down some stolen property. I found him seated at his desk with a stack of paperwork and a glass of cranberry juice. He had short brown hair, an oval face, and sad gray eyes. "Chief," I said, "what do you know about Dr. James P. White?"

"Not much. He's a chiropractor. Been in business here several years." He took a drink of cranberry juice and sat back in his chair.

"Where did he live before?"

"I don't know." He looked at me and looked at the paperwork. I couldn't tell for sure which he wanted to deal with, but I would have bet on the paperwork. I was just an interruption.

"Where did he go to school?"

"His ad in the paper says he went to Palmer in Davenport. Most chiropractors around here did."

"Uh-huh."

"Why all the questions, Scofield? Did he shoplift a box of Band-Aids or something?"

"Don't think so, Chief. I think he knows something about the murder of Jason King, but he wouldn't tell me. I tried to bluff him, but it didn't work. All it got me was a run-in with the big ape who drives him around." I didn't mention the part about the ear lobe.

The chief seemed more interested in this topic. He leaned forward and rested his elbows on the desk. "That would be little Bobby Kesler," he said. "Not very bright, but eager to please. Better not let him get hold of you if you want to keep your body parts attached."

"So I gathered."

"Bobby dropped out of school as soon as the law allowed. He never caught on to the idea that the letters on a page represented words."

"Another victim of the information age."

"He did six months for burglary when he was eighteen. It made him more cautious, but not smarter. White gave him the only job he ever had."

"How generous of him."

Metcalf grunted and took another drink of cranberry juice.

λ

After talking to Chief Metcalf, I checked into the Starlight Motel at the south end of town. I had a long shower and a short shave.

Then I went to the dining room for pancakes, orange juice, and a pot of coffee. Regeneration set in, and by the time I got back to my room, I had begun to resemble Michael Scofield again.

I opened the drapes and looked out at the abandoned freight yard across the street. Savanna was still an important rail center, but nothing like it once had been. It had plenty of automobiles and trucks, though. A constant stream of them rolled down Chicago Avenue.

I turned from the window, picked up the phone, and called the Palmer College of Chiropractic Medicine in Davenport. I asked to speak to someone with access to student records, and a woman with a mellifluous voice came on the line. "How may I help you?" she said.

"This is Michael Scofield," I said. "I'm calling to confirm that a Dr. James P. White is a graduate of your school."

"Just a moment please and I'll check that for you." There was a short pause. Then the mellifluous voice came on the line again. "Mr. Scofield?"

"Yes."

"Our records show that a James P. White graduated from Palmer fifteen years ago."

"Do you know where he went into practice and where he might be now?"

"Just a moment." Another pause. "Mr. Scofield?"

"Yes."

"Dr. White joined a practice in Chicago right after graduation."

"Did he subsequently move to Savanna, Illinois?"

"Our records don't show that, but we haven't had a new entry in his file for quite some time."

"What was the name of his office in Chicago?"

"The Broadway Chiropractic Clinic."

"Do you have a phone number for it?"

"No, I'm sorry. He must not have given us one."

"That's all right. Thank you."

"You're welcome."

With barely a pause, I called information for area 312. When Scofield gets a clue, he charges like a steam locomotive.

"What city please?"

"Chicago."

"Yes?"

"The Broadway Chiropractic Clinic."

Pause. Click, click. A mechanical voice came on the line with the number. I wrote it down, depressed and released the switch hook, and dialed again.

"Broadway Chiropractic Clinic," a female voice said.

"This is Michael Scofield from the Scofield Detective Agency in Davenport, Iowa," I said. "Could you connect me with Dr. White?"

This request elicited a brief pause. "I can't do that," she said, "but one of the other doctors could talk to you."

"No, I need to speak directly to Dr. White. When could I reach him?"

"I'm sorry, Mr. Scofield, but you can't reach him. Dr. White died ten years ago."

Chapter Twenty-Three

I sat by the phone for twenty minutes, trying to understand the strange career of Dr. James P. White. But no matter how long I thought about it, only one thing was certain: If he had died ten years before, it was too late to send flowers.

I waited until afternoon before going out to snoop around again. I didn't think I'd find anything, but I'd been wrong before. I checked out of the Starlight Motel, climbed into the Chevy, and drove back down Chicago Avenue.

Savanna is a pretty little town, laid out in a narrow, curving strip along the river. To the east, a bluff rises two hundred feet. To the west, the river lies only a few blocks from the foot of the bluff. Most of the town rests on this narrow strip of land between the bluff and the river, although a few streets angle tentatively up the steep slope.

At the south end of town, the bluff pulls back from the river, creating a wider strip of usable land. It's here that you find the abandoned freight yards visible from the Starlight Motel. Above the weeds and the rotting ties, an odd relic remains in use. A concrete viaduct built to carry a street over the rail yards now crosses a hazard that no longer exists, like a bridge over a dried-up river.

I drove slowly down Chicago Avenue, past St. John the Baptist Catholic Church, and turned right onto Main Street. The brick stores and office buildings on Main were erected in the late nineteenth century, at a time when the future still seemed to lie with the Savannas of the country. In fact, the future still looked pretty good in Savanna that afternoon, although I didn't know what was holding the local economy together. Tourism maybe. With its high, steel bridge reaching out from its wooded bluff to the long causeway on the opposite side of the river, Savanna was worth the trip.

I drove back to Dr. Brady-White's office, parked in front, and walked to the door. The "CLOSED" sign in the window came as no surprise. Just for sport, I tried the door. It was locked as tight as a towboat in January.

I got back into the Chevy and drove to the residential address listed for James P. White in the phone book. It was a white-clapboard Greek Revival house with Doric columns supporting a small porch. Chimneys rose above the roof at both the left and right gable ends. Side windows and a transom framed the front door. Brady-White had good taste in houses, if not in muscle-bound companions.

I walked up the sidewalk and climbed the steps to the porch. The house was dark, the shades drawn, the door locked. I knocked a couple of times just to stimulate my knuckles. No one came. I thought about walking around to the back and breaking in for a leisurely search, but Chief Metcalf knew I was looking for Dr. White and was bound to see the connection if anyone reported the break-in.

To bring the day's tour to a conclusion, I drove back to Sabula and parked in front of Brady-White's apartment. The Pontiac was nowhere in sight. I walked over to the front entrance and went into the building's small foyer, where a row of mailboxes faced the door. None of the boxes belonged to anyone named White, Brady, Burns, or Kesler.

I knocked on the door of apartment 1-A, and an elderly man came to the door. "Excuse me, sir," I said. "Do you know if Dr. James P. White lives in this building?"

"Dr. White? No. No one by that name lives here." He looked at me as if I were about as smart as a chuck roast. "If you need a doctor, you'd better go over to Savanna. They have plenty of doctors over there."

"Thank you, I'll do that."

"You're welcome." He closed the door, and the lock clicked. I didn't knock on any of the other doors. One medical referral was enough for the day. I got into the car, drove across the causeway to the Iowa shore, and turned south toward home.

↟

D. D. Palmer, the founder of chiropractic medicine, was full of ideas, some his own, some borrowed from others. His critics often called his ideas quackery, but this never stopped him from putting them into operation. At different times in his career, he practiced phrenology, magnetic healing, and spiritualism.

But Palmer's most successful idea was chiropractic medicine, which he created in 1895. He then set out to advertise this new discipline, using tactics he had developed earlier in a mail-order business. He even founded a college in Davenport to teach his new form of healing.

With the fruits of all this effort still very visible in the Quad Cities, I had no trouble finding a chiropractor to answer a few questions. As soon as I got back to the office, I called Nick Panagakis, an old high school chum. "Nick," I said, "how are things popping?"

"Not bad, Mike," he said. "How's the private eye biz?"

"Not so hot right now. I have more questions than answers about the Jason King murder, which is why I'm calling you. One of the guys I'm investigating claims to be a chiropractor, but I have my doubts. My question is, would it be possible for someone to pass himself off as a chiropractor without first going to school to learn the trade?"

"Anything's possible, but it's not very likely. First you have to know how the human body operates. Then you have to know how to treat it according to the principles of chiropractic science. Your man would have to learn all this somehow."

"Forgive me for mentioning it, but some people say it's not a real science anyway. So why would it be so hard fake it?"

"I know what some people say, Mike. Most of them write the letters 'M.D.' after their names. I just don't happen to agree with them, although I admit that I have a vested interest in the business. My children need music lessons and high-tech shoes. But whether it's a legitimate science or not, you still have to know how to do it before you start a practice. Even if you're only going through the motions, you still have to know what the motions are. See what I mean?"

"Perfectly. Thanks."

"My pleasure."

"You'd better get cracking."

"Thanks, Mike. I will."

I hung up and paced for a while. Slowly, very slowly, I was accumulating information. You couldn't call it "evidence" yet, because I didn't yet know for sure what it proved about the death of Jason King. This worried me. What if my information refused to turn into evidence? I paced some more. Pacing had a calming effect on me, but it didn't bring any revelations. I paced for twenty minutes. Then Carlos walked in.

"Carlos," I said, "it's good to see you." I sat down and motioned for him to do the same. "How'd you know I was here?"

"I tried to call you and the line was busy."

"Excellent deduction. What's been happening since I talked to you last night?"

"Karl Deutsch died this morning."

"He died?"

"Yes. About eleven-thirty."

"That's a surprise, though I can't say I'm really sad. My ribs still hurt from the kicks he gave them. What did he die from?"

"I don't know. No one would say. There's going to be an autopsy. I called Dr. Cook's office. He wasn't there, but his secretary said that Deutsch was too young to just get sick and die."

"Secretaries always seem to know these things, don't they? By the way, you don't look so hot yourself. Are you all right?" He looked haggard.

"I'm okay. I just didn't get any sleep last night."

"Why not?" I could guess, but I didn't say it.

"I was looking for Kathy. I still haven't seen a thing of her. Now that Deutsch is dead, I don't know where to look next."

"Why don't you go home and go to bed? That's what I plan to do. After a good night's sleep, maybe things will start to sort themselves out." I had no idea if things would start to sort themselves out or not, but I was trying to reassure the boy. Now all we needed was someone to reassure me.

≬

I don't know if Carlos got a good night's sleep, but I did. I rolled out at nine o'clock the next morning and had breakfast at Vigo's Cafe. The coffee was still free. I paid for the food and walked to the city library.

The Davenport Public Library is a white, box-like building with about as much character as a refrigerator. I liked the old library better, but no one asked me before they tore it down. I walked inside and began a digital search of the *Chicago Tribune*. I looked at the obituaries for a six-month period approximately ten years before. It didn't take long to find the one I wanted:

> Dr. James Patrick White, 28, a Chicago chiropractor, died Monday at his home in Evanston. After graduation from the Palmer College of Chiropractic in Davenport, Iowa, he joined the practice of Drs. David Stein, Margaret Walsh, and Peter O'Brien at the Broadway Chiropractic Clinic in Chicago. He is survived by his parents, Mr. and Mrs. Thomas White; two sisters, Colleen White and Joan Fogarty; and one brother, Edward. Services will be held at 9:30 AM Thursday at the Trevor Funeral Home in Evanston. Mass will be at 10 AM Thursday in St. Mary's Church, Evanston.

I wondered why Dr. White had died so young, but the obituary provided no answer to that question. Other questions remained as well. I had more reading to do.

Starting with the month one year prior to White's death, I began looking through every issue of the *Tribune*. It was tedious work, and after the first thirty minutes I thought I was going blind. I finally reached the date of White's death without having found anything useful. With the spirit of my pioneer ancestors, I took a break for coffee and pastry. Then I struggled on.

Finally, I found something. Six months after White's death, an article concerning Dr. Peter O'Brien had appeared, the same Peter O'Brien associated with the Broadway Chiropractic Clinic. The article stated that O'Brien had been accused of real-estate fraud, having sold property on Lake Michigan north of the city at a point where the lake was rapidly eroding the shoreline. Water and real estate. Where had I heard that theme before?

O'Brien had convinced the buyer that the state was planning to build a floodwall to protect the shore, when, in fact, the state had no such plans at all. He had even shown the buyer some documents that allegedly proved the state's intention to construct the wall.

Nothing more about O'Brien appeared in the paper until about one month later, when an article reported that he had suddenly disappeared without a trace. His disappearance had come at an opportune time for him, since the Lake County Prosecutor's Office was about to issue an indictment. I didn't bother to look for any more articles. I was already certain that O'Brien had never returned.

Chapter Twenty-Four

To confirm my suspicions about the disappearance of Dr. Peter O'Brien, I went to my office after lunch and called the Lake County, Illinois, Prosecutor's Office. An assistant state's attorney named Priscilla Novak dug out the files and returned my call.

"We never found him," she said. "He left no trail when he fled, and we never got a good lead on him afterwards. We don't have the resources to look very long for someone like this. The best we could hope for would be a tip from the public. You don't have a tip from the public for us, do you, Mr. Scofield?"

"I'm afraid not," I said. "Not yet anyway. Do you know if Peter O'Brien was his real name?"

"We don't know. That was one of the problems with this case. There are plenty of Peter O'Briens in the world, but we were never able to match any of their histories with this Peter O'Brien. My personal suspicion is that the name was an alias. What do you think?"

"I think you're probably right. Thanks for your help."

"You're welcome. You will remember to call me if you find out anything, won't you?"

"Absolutely." I hung up.

⸙

I stood at the window for a while, looking at the vacant building across the street. If I ever had the money to move to a classier address, the thing I would miss the most would be the building across the street. There's something about an abandoned building, its empty windows gaping at the world, its secrets hiding in dark corners.

Some people think that old abandoned buildings are eyesores. They want to see them torn down to make way for parking lots and Quiktrips. But I like having them around to remind us of our past, with all its false promises, vain hopes, and occasional triumphs. I wondered how long this building would last before someone pulled it down and erected a monument to his own tiny imagination.

Down on the sidewalk, a wino came lurching around the corner of the building and spat in the gutter. Winos in Davenport have a sense of social responsibility. They don't spit on the sidewalk unless they can't make it to the gutter. I turned from the window, went back to the phone, and called the Broadway Chiropractic Clinic in Chicago. The same woman as the day before answered the phone.

"I need to speak to either Dr. Stein or Dr. Walsh," I said.

"Dr. Walsh is out for the day, but I can ask Dr. Stein to call you back," she said.

I said that would be fine and hung up. I didn't like waiting, but what else could I do? I got up and went back to the window. It had started to rain—a hard, steady rain. With its face soaked, the building across the street seemed even more mysterious. I still liked it, but I had to admit that there was such a thing as too much mystery. Like the mystery of Dr. Brady-White, and now, Dr. O'Brien. I went to the fridge and pulled out a bottle of Beck's Dark. Time to get the old synapses firing in sync. I sat down and took a swallow.

Four beers later the old synapses were still sputtering along, still not in sync. By now, though, it didn't seem to matter. And by now the building across the street held more hidden meanings than all the movies of Ingmar Bergman. Finally, the phone rang. It was Dr. Stein. I hoped I didn't sound like a drunken detective.

"Dr. Stein," I said, "what can you tell me about Peter O'Brien?"

"What would you like to know?" he said. His tone was reserved, guarded.

"I understand that he disappeared after being charged with real-estate fraud. Is there anything more you can tell me about that?"

"I don't think so. You don't work for a newspaper, do you?"

"No, I don't. I'm a private detective working for the Morco drugstore chain. I'm investigating a murder that occurred at one of Morco's stores, and I think that O'Brien may have information about it."

"I see. Well, I don't know anything about that. All I know is that he worked here for about five years, got in trouble with the law, and disappeared."

"Do you know where he was from?"

"He said he was from Cincinnati, Ohio."

"Was he married?"

"Not that I know of."

"Was Peter O'Brien his real name?"

"I assumed it was, but I can't be certain. People will tell you anything."

"Where did he take his training?"

"At the Indianapolis College of Chiropractic Medicine. At least, that's what he said. He had his diploma hanging on the wall like everyone else in the clinic."

"Do you think he was really a chiropractor," I asked, "or was that just a front for his other activities?"

This question elicited a long silence. Finally, Dr. Stein said, slowly and deliberately, "Are you sure you're not working for a newspaper?"

"I promise you that I'm not working for a newspaper. Why do you ask?"

"Mr. Scofield, I don't know if you're aware of it or not, but chiropractic medicine has had a long and difficult history of trying to prove that it is a legitimate science and a legitimate method of treating illness. The very idea that someone could practice chiropractic medicine without extensive training threatens the reputation of all chiropractors. Do you understand what I mean?"

"Yes, perfectly. I have no desire to threaten your profession or embarrass you in any way whatsoever. Nothing that you tell me will ever appear in the press. I can promise you that. All I want to do is find out who murdered a Morco employee named Jason King. That is my only interest in Peter O'Brien and his medical practice." I said all this with as much sincerity as four bottles of Beck's Dark could stimulate. I waited to see if he'd buy it.

After a pause, Dr. Stein, still speaking slowly and carefully, said, "After O'Brien disappeared, I made a few phone calls. I found that a man named Peter O'Brien had graduated from the Indianapolis College of Chiropractic Medicine, but I also found that he'd been killed in a car wreck a year later, which was something the people at the school didn't know until I informed them. I came to the conclusion that the man who worked here had assumed the identity of the real Peter O'Brien."

"Did you ever find out the real identity of the man who called himself Peter O'Brien?"

"I made a couple of attempts, but I never got anywhere, so I gave up. I knew all I needed to know anyway, once I found out that O'Brien was an impostor."

"Do the authorities know this?"

"They must. If I could find out, so could they. They came by and cleaned out his files, which reminds me of something else. I looked at his license and some other documents before the police took them. I couldn't tell for sure, but I think they were fakes. With modern printing equipment, it's not all that hard to create your own credentials."

"You're absolutely right. I have another question."

"Go ahead."

"What did O'Brien look like?"

"He was blond, blue-eyed, good looking. All the women wanted him as their doctor. He was in his twenties when he started here."

"How tall?"

"About five-nine, five-ten."

I finished writing all this down. "Is there anything else you can tell me?" I said.

"Not really. That's all I know."

"Thank you, Dr. Stein. You've been a great help. And if you ever want to go into the detective business, give me a call."

He laughed sincerely at this. "Thank you, Mr. Scofield," he said. "I'll remember that."

ϟ

I hung up, turned my swivel chair toward the window, and watched the rain pour down. Priscilla Novak at the Lake County Prosecutor's Office had not been entirely candid with me. She had left out parts of the story I needed to know. That's why a private investigator has to gather his own information. You can't depend on the police. They're not obliged to tell you anything, not even the price of rhubarb in Peoria.

It was mid-afternoon by now, rapidly approaching late afternoon, too late to start anything new for the day. I went to the fridge for my fifth Beck's Dark. Germans, as I've said before, make the best beer. Beer is their redeeming quality. It makes up for sauerkraut, lederhosen, and organ music. I drank two more bottles. By the time I finished the second, I was ready to give long testimonials for the German Tourist Bureau.

It was still raining. I found a battered umbrella somewhere and managed to get it open. I locked up and went slowly, very slowly, down the stairs to Fourth Street. From there I walked over to LeClaire Park to look at the river.

The river was still there. Towboats were pushing barges upstream and down, oblivious to the rain. Jobs on the Mississippi have always attracted people living along its banks. When you take one of those jobs and go on board your first riverboat, you're performing an act referred to by river people as going "over the levee." And once you do that, they say, you can never really come back. You can come back physically, but not spiritually.

I had known many men and a few women who had gone over the levee, and I had to agree with that old belief. Some of those men and women had subsequently left their riverboat jobs for something more secure, more lucrative, or safer, but all of them still wished they were on the river. As I stood in the rain in LeClaire Park, drunk on German beer, with an old umbrella that wouldn't stay open, I imagined that I knew what river people thought and felt about the Mississippi.

Then I threw away the umbrella and walked home in the rain.

Chapter Twenty-Five

I waited until the next afternoon to contact Dr. Cook, the Scott County medical examiner. By then he would have had enough time to complete his autopsy on Karl Deutsch. I called his office, but had to wait for him to call me back. Doctors can't be programmed to receive calls, only to make them. It has something to do with neural pathways and large bank accounts. Finally, he returned my call. "Dr. Cook," I said, "how's life in the morgue?"

"Deadly. What can I do for you, Scofield?"

"I'm curious about the early death of Karl Deutsch. What can you tell me?"

"He died from cancer of the liver, which probably resulted from long-term use of anabolic-androgenic steroids."

"That's the price you pay for a healthy body."

"Actually, his life could have been saved if he'd gone to see a doctor a long time ago instead of playing the tough guy."

"Is it possible that his death was hastened along by someone? Could his symptoms have provided a cover for murder?"

He paused, but for only a moment. "I don't think so. I saw no evidence of anything else, although I did notice signs of a recent blow to the stomach."

"Oh?" This was a complication I hadn't thought of.

"It looked as if someone had hit him with a small, blunt object right in the belly. But that didn't kill him or even injure him seriously."

"I see." What a relief.

"Why did you think he might have been murdered?"

"I'm investigating the death of Jason King, and every time I blow my nose somebody gets killed."

"Stop blowing your nose."

"Thanks, Doctor. Good idea."

"You're welcome, Scofield."

Upon reflection, I found that in at least one respect, the death of Karl Deutsch bothered me. Now it would be even more difficult to find either Max Brady-White or Kathy Dove-Linn whenever I needed to, not that finding them had been all that easy before. Deutsch had never been eager to give out information about them, but there was always the chance, while he was still alive, that he might lead Carlos or me to them when necessary. Now that chance had died.

I sat and pondered my options for a while. I didn't have many, so the exercise didn't tax my brain. The shadowy past of Brady-White-O'Brien suggested one possibility. Kathy Dove-Linn had sought treatment at the Prairie Flower Chiropractic Clinic in

Moline. Why couldn't I? And who would my doctor be? I had a good idea. I looked up the number and dialed.

"Prairie Flower Chiropractic Clinic," said a woman's melodious voice. Her voice reminded me of the woman at the Palmer College of Chiropractic. Maybe they were sisters.

"Hello," I said. "My name is Robert Hunter, and I have a terrible backache. Could you squeeze me in this afternoon?"

"I'm sorry, Mr. Hunter. Dr. Barber is all booked up for the rest of the afternoon, but he could see you tomorrow morning."

"All right, I guess that'll have to do."

"Would ten o'clock be okay?"

"That would be fine."

"All right," she said melodiously. "We'll see you then." She had such a nice voice that my back felt better already.

‏

The next morning, I drove across the Memorial Bridge to the Prairie Flower Chiropractic Clinic on Sixth Avenue in Moline. Carlos was already there, parked a few doors short of the clinic. If my suspicion was correct, I would soon need his help. If Brady-White-O'Brien-Barber tried to disappear again, Carlos would be there to take up the chase. If Jutjaw was present and got his big hands on me, Carlos would be there to sweep up the pieces.

Shortly before ten I walked into the waiting room of the clinic, where I learned that the melodious voice belonged to an attractive young black woman. "Do you have a sister who works at Palmer College?" I asked.

"Yes I do," she said, smiling.

"Your voices sound exactly alike."

"That's what everyone says." She handed me a form and a ball-point pen. I sat down and filled out the form with all kinds of information about Robert Hunter, all of which was about as true as the life history of Dr. White-O'Brien-Barber.

The woman then ushered me into an examination room and instructed me to get undressed and put on a hospital gown in anticipation of Dr. Barber's appearance. I smiled and nodded agreement, and the woman left.

I had no intention of putting on the gown. When Dr. Barber walked in, I planned to be fully clothed and fully armed. I took my automatic out of its holster, cocked it, left the safety off, and slipped it into my jacket pocket, where I kept it firmly in my right hand.

I stayed on my feet, facing the door. My stomach tightened. My heart raced. I was ready, but ready for what? I hoped Jutjaw had the day off. I heard someone stop outside the door, then walk on. A few moments later, someone approached the door again, shuffled some papers, and knocked. The last chiropractor I'd seen had given me a surprise. This time I'd give him a surprise. The door swung open.

I started to take the automatic out of my pocket, then stopped. Standing in the door was a young black man wearing a white jacket, a red silk tie, and a friendly smile. He closed the door and stepped toward me. "Good morning, Mr. Hunter," he said, extending his right hand. "How are you today?"

I shook hands. Fortunately, I remembered to let go of the gun before taking my hand out of my jacket pocket. Once again, the surprise was on me. Dr. White-O'Brien was not Dr. Barber. "Good morning, Doctor," I said. "I have a backache."

Dr. Barber asked me a series of questions about my symptoms, and I made up a series of answers. The answers were so convincing that I almost believed them. Dr. Barber seemed to believe them, too. Now I felt embarrassed that I hadn't put on the stupid gown, but Dr. Barber was too polite to mention it. After he finished with the questions, he said, "Why don't you get undressed and put on the gown and I'll come back in a few minutes." He walked out and closed the door.

Now what? I had bluffed my way in. Now, to avoid suspicion, I would have to bluff my way through the whole process. I took off my jacket and hid the holster in the left pocket. The pistol was still in the right pocket. Then I took off the rest of my clothes and put on the gown. It's bad enough to go through this ritual when you're really sick. To do it when you're healthy is even worse.

Dr. Barber returned a few minutes later and directed me onto the examination table, a long padded affair where you lie on your stomach and rest your nose and mouth in a contoured hole. The treatment may not help you, but at least you won't suffocate.

Dr. Barber began the exam, running his fingers slowly along my spine. This procedure took a while, as he felt each vertebra in relation to its neighbors. Occasionally, he tapped gently with his fingers. Sometimes he placed one hand flat on my spine and lightly struck the back of that hand with his other hand. After completing this process, during which I almost fell asleep, he said, "You have a subluxation in the lumbar region of your spine. Just relax while I massage for a while."

These instructions were unnecessary. I was already so relaxed that I felt like a rag doll in a gentle whirlpool. After several minutes of massaging, Dr. Barber put his hands together and gave my lower spine a firm, short push—what chiropractors call a "high-velocity thrust." My backbone popped like a barrage of champagne corks. I had felt perfectly healthy when I first lay down on the table, and now I felt so good that I thought I might never die. Scofield the immortal. Dr. Barber had achieved the most successful cure of a nonexistent ailment in medical history.

He manipulated my spine a short while longer, then brought the session to a close. It had taken about twenty-five minutes. "How do you feel?" he said.

"Terrific. Do your patients become immortal?"

"It's too soon to tell. I've only been in business for two years. Ask me a hundred years from now."

"I'll do that. Be sure to keep score in the meantime."

"I will."

"By the way, do you know a Dr. White in Savanna, Illinois? He's a chiropractor, too."

He thought for a moment. "No, I don't think I do. Why do you ask?"

"Just curious. You're very good at this, by the way. If you don't mind my asking, where did you take your training?"

"At Palmer in Davenport. I grew up here in Moline, so it was very convenient for me."

We exchanged a few more pleasantries, during which Dr. Barber revealed that the young woman with the melodious voice was his wife, who was also a native of Moline. I thanked him for his help, and he left the room. I got dressed, putting my automatic back into its holster and the holster back under my arm. Then I walked out to the waiting room and paid Ms. Barber in cash. I thought this would be best, since I didn't have any checks with the name "Robert Hunter" on them.

Ms. Barber told me to call again if I had any more problems. I said goodbye and headed for the door. On the way out I noticed a young woman reading a copy of *National Geographic*. The animal on the cover was a panda bear. The woman holding the magazine was Kathy Dove.

ʎ

I didn't think she had noticed me, so I turned my face in the other direction and went on out the door. Carlos was still sitting in his car, looking like something about to erupt. I slipped into the seat beside him, and the volcano exploded.

"Did you see her, Mike? It was Kathy, Kathy Dove. Or Linn, I don't know which. She looked good. She looked great. I wonder where she's been. You must've seen her. She just went in a few minutes ago. I think she—"

"Carlos."

"She—"

"Carlos!"

"Yes?"

"Stop and take a breath, Carlos. You never outgrow your need for air."

"Okay." He did as I said, breathing deeply a few times. I'm sure it saved his life.

"I saw her on the way out," I said. "She looks just fine. Running into her like this is all right, too. Let's wait until she comes out, and we'll see where she leads us. Let's not get excited and blow it, okay?" I looked at him to make sure he was paying attention. He was. "I met Dr. Barber, and he had me convinced he was strictly legitimate, but now I'm not so sure. It seems like too much of a coincidence that Kathy keeps showing up here."

"What's Barber look like?" Carlos said.

"Young. Black. Good looking. Has a trim mustache and short hair. About five-eight with a slight build. You know him?"

"Did he grow up here?"

"That's what he said. So did his wife. She works with him."

"I don't know him personally, but I know who he is. Nice guy. Or that's how he seems."

Our discussion of Dr. Barber had a calming effect on Carlos. He was now able to remember that he was a private detective and that we were trying to solve a murder. I left him sitting there and walked back to my car, which was parked several spaces behind his.

We sat for another twenty minutes. The sun was glaring off the cars in front of me. I put on my dark glasses, but my head and neck began to hurt anyway. If this continued much longer,

I'd have to see a chiropractor. Finally, Carlos called me on my cell phone. "She's coming out, Mike. A cab's waiting in front."

"Okay." I started the car.

"They're moving, Mike."

"Got it." I waited a little longer, then pulled away from the curb. The cab was already a block and a half in front, with Carlos a block behind it. I followed at a respectful distance for a while. Then I passed Carlos, and he followed me at a respectful distance for a while.

We tailed the cab all the way through Moline in this fashion, first with Carlos in front, then me, then Carlos, then me—just so Kathy wouldn't look back and see the same car every time. Finally, we reached East Moline. After a few blocks, the cab turned right onto a side street and drove a few more blocks to a little gray-green bungalow in a quiet neighborhood. Hardwood trees and a picket fence sheltered the bungalow. I wondered what foul eggs little Kathy and her friends might be hatching in this peaceful setting.

I knew it would be almost impossible to drag Carlos away from the object of his infatuation, so I suggested that he take the first shift of our stakeout at the bungalow. He promised to call me if anything happened, and I drove back to the office to throw away the mail and erase the answering machine.

I worked at my desk for a while, then got on the phone to Vic Domino. "Vic," I said, "it's time to try the shotgun approach. I'm going to give you a list of names, and I want you to dig up all the dirt you can on them. Use all the resources at your disposal."

All the resources at Vic's disposal included several data bases that he was legally entitled to use and many more that he was illegally entitled to use. My list of names included Jason King, Rebecca King, cashier Tracy Gibbs, pharmacist Brian Walker, Max Brady (with all his aliases), desk clerk Fred Hutz, Karl Deutsch, Bobby "Jutjaw" Kesler, Joseph Meiers, drug dealer Richard Miner, Dr. David Stein, Dr. Margaret Walsh, George Mann, Grandfather Albert Vox, Kathy Dove-Linn, Dr. and Ms. Barber, the lovely Carlotta, and the big man himself, William Morrison. I didn't give Vic my own name because I was relatively sure of my innocence. I was even more sure of Carlos's innocence, so I left his name off the list, too.

"This is going to cost you," Vic said.

"What doesn't?" I said. It's easy to be cavalier about money when someone else is paying the bill.

\

At seven o'clock that evening, I drove back to East Moline, and Carlos joined me in the Chevy. "Anything to report?" I asked.

"Not much," he said. "About three hours after you left, another cab showed up and Kathy got in. I followed her to the downtown Morco in Davenport. She went inside and the cab waited. I stopped across the street and watched through the front windows. Kathy picked up a prescription, came right back out, and took the cab back here."

"Did she stop and pay?"

"No, she just came straight out. The cashier was looking at her, so it must have been all right."

"Maybe. Who was the cashier?"

"Tracy Gibbs."

"Who was the pharmacist?"

"Brian Walker."

"My, my, my." I sat back in the seat and pondered.

"What are you thinking?" Carlos said.

"I'm thinking how convenient it would be for Max Brady if little Kathy picked up his stolen drugs for him."

"She wouldn't do that." He sounded offended.

"Maybe she would and maybe she wouldn't. She might not even know what drugs she was getting or what Brady would do with them."

"Brady couldn't make enough on the drugs stolen from one store. Someone would notice if a lot disappeared."

"Someone already did. Jason King. Besides that, Brady wouldn't rely on only one source. He'd have lots of others as well, different sources for different drugs. That's why Deutsch was willing to meet you at the repair sheds in Silvis. I'm sure he and Brady were happy whenever someone dropped more drugs in their laps."

"But that doesn't mean the drugs Kathy picked up this afternoon were for Brady." Carlos didn't want to admit that Kathy might be involved in the illegal drug trade, even if she didn't know what she was doing. "Maybe she charged them. That would explain why she didn't stop to pay."

"She'd still have to stop at the cash register, Carlos. That's the way they do it at Morco. She didn't stop because she knew that Tracy didn't expect her to."

He thought for a moment. "Yeah," he said. He couldn't deny what he'd seen for himself.

I finally told him not to worry about it. I was there to watch the house while he took a break, not to turn Kathy over to the police. It came as no surprise that he didn't want to take a break. He wanted to stay close to Kathy in case he needed to rescue her from someone or something. I finally convinced him to go get something to eat. He went back to his car and drove away.

It was a crisp, quiet fall night in East Moline. The stars shone down. A street light threw the shadows of giant maples onto the clapboard siding of bungalows and foursquares. Leaves lay in piles along the curb.

Half an hour after Carlos's departure, a dark-blue Pontiac pulled into the driveway beside the bungalow. The first person out of the car was Mr. Jutjaw, Bobby Kesler. A bandage covered his left ear. He looked around, then said something to someone in the car. Max Brady emerged from the back seat, followed quickly by a young woman with dark hair. I couldn't see her well enough to recognize her. She linked arms with Brady, and all three people entered the house through a side door.

Brady's arrival with Jutjaw didn't surprise me. Now that Karl Deutsch had gone to the big drugstore in paradise, someone else would have to baby-sit with Kathy Dove-Linn. Carlos Lorca would have liked the job, but he didn't meet the qualifications. His IQ was too high.

Chapter Twenty-Six

Carlos returned about an hour after leaving. He parked a few spaces back and walked up to the Chevy. He was well fed, full of coffee, and glad to be back. "Carlos," I said, "the gang's all here—Kathy, Brady, Jutjaw, and a woman that I couldn't quite identify." It was too dark in the car to see Carlos, so I kept my eyes on the house as I talked. "The question is, what do we do now?"

"Confront them? Call the police?"

"No, I've already confronted them, for all the good it did me, and it's still too early for the police. We could make a good case against Brady for fraud, drug dealing, practicing medicine without a license, and bad manners—but not murder. And murder's what we're really interested in. We have to find out who killed Jason King. That's what Morrison is paying us for. And I wouldn't mind finding out who killed Joseph Meiers while we're at it."

"What if Deutsch killed them? Now that he's dead, how will we ever know?"

"That's a good question. It's been banging around in my head ever since he died. He may have killed them both, but we can't assume it."

"Brady could have done it himself."

"Perhaps. Or maybe Jutjaw killed them. Or maybe all three did it together. I wouldn't put it past any of them."

Carlos waited as a car drove by, then said, "But why would any of them use a butcher knife?"

"Another good question. Who would use a knife when there's so much firepower available? It's not all that easy to kill someone by stabbing him in the chest, unless he knows and trusts you, or unless you're very strong. The victim would at least put up his hands to defend himself, but neither King nor Meiers had wounds on his hands or arms."

"But both Deutsch and Jutjaw were strong enough to overpower them."

"True, but the use of a knife, especially the same kind of knife each time, suggests that we're looking for a crazy man."

"Like who?"

"I don't know. Jutjaw is stupid and cunning, but probably not crazy. The same was true of Deutsch. On the surface, Brady seems sane, but his use of bodyguards, multiple residences, and aliases suggests a streak of paranoia. On the other hand, given the kind of life he leads, maybe his paranoia is justified."

A motorcycle went by, filling the night with its adolescent racket. "So what shall we do?" Carlos said.

"Wait and watch," I said, "and hope that Morrison doesn't withdraw our funding."

Both of us had run out of anything to say. We sat there in the darkness, watching the bungalow. Time marched on. Slowly.

Nothing happened until Jutjaw suddenly came through the side door and ushered Kathy into the back seat of the Pontiac.

"I'll follow them," Carlos said.

"Stay in touch," I said, "and don't try to be a hero."

"Sure, Mike," he said as he jumped out and turned toward his car. I wasn't confident that he would follow my orders, but there's a limit to what you can make another human being do, especially if he's only twenty-one years old.

Ɣ

The next six hours passed about as quickly as the Stone Age. No one entered the bungalow. No one left. An upstairs light went off at midnight, which from my point of view was the main event of the evening.

A little after two in the morning, the dark-blue Pontiac pulled into the driveway and stopped by the side door. Kathy and Jutjaw wasted no time getting into the house, and thirty seconds later, Carlos pulled into the space behind me with his lights already off. He walked up, opened the door, and hopped in. "Carlos," I said, "you promised to stay in touch."

"Sorry, Mike, I was too busy." He sounded pleased with himself.

"Doing what?"

"Watching Kathy."

"I'll bet. Tell me about it."

"Jutjaw took her straight to the Gentleman's Retreat. I waited a little while, then went in to keep an eye on things."

"Carlos, if you don't stop hanging around that place, you're going to grow hair on your palms."

"It's worth it."

"I hope you had a good time. Did you get your money's worth?"

"Oh, yes," he said with wide-eyed inflection. "Worth every cent."

"Did she follow any particular theme for the night?" I asked. The conversation had taken a voyeuristic turn, but I was too tired to turn it in a more spiritual direction.

"Sports."

"Go on."

"First she came in as a football player. Starting with her helmet, she took off everything but her cleats."

"No kidding?"

"Swear to god. Guess what she took off last."

"Her underpants?"

"Nope, her jockstrap."

"Of course. How stupid of me."

"Next she came in as a boxer."

"A boxer?"

"Right. She shadow-boxed for a few minutes, then pounded the hell out of a punching bag."

"I'm afraid to ask, but how was she dressed?"

"Gloves only."

"Thank god. I was afraid she might have left the cleats on."

"For the last show, she came out as a jockey."

"Hold it right there, Carlos. I've heard enough."

"It's not as bad as it sounds, Mike."

"I don't care. It's hard enough to think pure thoughts, and you're making it even more difficult."

"It was a good show."

"Glad you liked it. Now I want you to stay here while I go somewhere and sit in a tub of ice water."

"Sure, Mike, anything you say."

Carlos went back to his car, and I drove to Gene's Diner. I didn't sit in a tub of water, but I did drink a glass or two of the stuff, plus almost a quart of coffee. When I got back to the bungalow, Carlos joined me in the Chevy. He was barely awake. I told him to take a nap, and he fell asleep in about half a second. Two hours later, I woke him up and I took a nap. By eight o'clock the next morning, I was wide awake and ready for trouble. I needed a shave, but I wasn't in the army, so nobody cared.

At a quarter to nine, Jutjaw came out the door with the dark-haired woman, and both got into the Pontiac. Jutjaw backed out of the driveway and drove off. I started the Chevy, and Carlos got out to walk back to his car. I pulled away from the curb and followed the Pontiac, which was already about a block in front of me.

Jutjaw took the Memorial Bridge across the Mississippi and drove down East River Drive to Davenport. When he got downtown, he turned right, drove two blocks, and turned right on Third Street. Suddenly it hit me. The Empire Building. He was taking her to the Empire Building, which contained, among other things, the offices of George Mann and the Property Management Associates. I parked half a block away and watched her go inside. Even though it was Saturday, she was dressed for business in a black dress and high heels. Jutjaw drove off, and I climbed out of the Chevy.

I thought about going right upstairs and asking her some embarrassing questions in front of George Mann, but I decided to wait. I popped into a café across the street and camped at a table beside the window, where I demolished a plate of scrambled eggs and fried potatoes, a large orange juice, and several cups of coffee, all while keeping the Empire Building clearly in view.

The neoclassical Empire Building is one of the most impressive structures in Davenport. Its white limestone facade gives it a look of solidity without being ponderous. A Greek temple forms the upper story, with a clock tower atop that. The clock tower reminds you of an age before digital watches and time-temperature bank signs. The interior of the building is just as impressive as the exterior. The ground-level banking room rises from a tiled floor to a vaulted ceiling, complete with a cathedral-like painting of heroic pioneers.

By ten-thirty, I had drunk enough coffee to float a grain barge. Finally, Mann's dark-haired secretary emerged from the Empire Building and started down the sidewalk. I left some money on the table, hurried out the door, and caught up with the woman a block away. "Excuse me," I said. "I'm a Hollywood talent scout, and I think you have a future in Technicolor."

She stopped and turned around as if she almost believed me. Disappointment came quickly. "Oh, it's you," she said.

"Who'd you expect? Sam Goldwyn?" She gave me a blank look, and I realized that Sam Goldwyn meant about as much to her as Sam Spade. "Sorry," I said. "Wrong decade."

Her blank look deepened. "What are you talking about?"

"Never mind. Let's talk about Max Brady. You remember him don't you?"

This startled her. Her pretty face was easier to read than a stop sign. "I don't know anyone by that name," she said.

"That's too bad. You just spent the night with him. You should ask a guy's name before you let him take off your underwear."

"You're crazy." She spun around and walked away. I followed. People were staring, but I didn't care. "Leave me alone or I'll call the police," she said.

"Excellent idea," I said. "Call the FBI while you're at it. They'd love to ask you some questions about Max. Just a second, I'll lend you some change."

"Leave me alone." She walked faster.

"Then you can explain to your boss how you fed information to Max during negotiations for the River Village Addition." I trotted around in front of her and blocked her escape. She stopped and glared at me. "That's what you did, isn't it?" I said. "You put George Mann at quite a disadvantage by telling Max Brady in advance what Mann was prepared to offer. That bothers me, because it also put my boss at a disadvantage. But what bothers me most of all are the murders of Jason King and Joe Meiers. Max was responsible for those, too, and I'll bet you know everything about them. You'd better tell me what you know if you want to avoid being charged as an accessory to murder. People around here are getting sick of all the dead bodies, and a jury won't give a shit how blue your eyes are."

I was shouting by now, and quite a crowd had gathered to watch the performance. Sam Goldwyn would have been proud. Sam Spade would have been proud, too. The dark-haired secretary had a different opinion. She pushed by me and went on down the street. I was tired of chasing her, and I had finished my lines, so I let her go. The crowd began to dissolve, and I started back toward the Empire Building. The Property Management Associates were in for a shock.

Chapter Twenty-Seven

George Mann's jaw dropped like a sandbag. "My god," he said. "I never would have guessed."

"I'm sure you wouldn't," I said.

Mann sat behind his desk, slowly shaking his head. It wasn't even noon yet, but he looked very tired. "No wonder Brady held his ground on his last offer," he said. "He knew exactly what Morrison was willing to pay."

"Did the secretary have access to all that information?"

"I'm afraid so. She kept the files. I trusted her with everything."

"How long has she worked here?"

"About a year."

"Did she have good references?"

"Yes, but I never checked them. They could be entirely fictitious for all I know." He turned to the side and looked out the window at the Mississippi. "I guess it must be obvious why I hired her." He turned back toward me. I nodded. "It adds a certain amount of credibility to a business if you have an attractive secretary. I hired her for her appearance and nothing else." He looked down. "I wonder what other information she's been giving to Max Brady."

I didn't say anything. Mann didn't look like such a smart businessman right then, and I didn't want to rub it in. "I feel like a fool," he said.

"What's her name?" I asked.

"Rita Vermilion."

"Where does she live?"

"East Moline."

"Could you give me the address?" He looked it up for me and I wrote it down. It just happened to be the address of the bungalow that Carlos and I had watched all night. I looked at Mann. "Thanks," I said.

An earnest look had settled on his face. "You're not going to tell Morrison about this, are you?"

"I don't know. It depends on whether or not it has anything to do with Jason King's murder. That's my only interest in Max Brady and Rita Vermilion."

He nodded. "I understand."

"But the next time you're about to hire an attractive secretary, you might try something."

"What's that?"

"Get yourself a private detective to check her out."

⅄

I went down to the Chevy and called Carlos. I assumed he was still watching the bungalow, and I didn't want him to get lonely.

"Mike," he said, "I just tried to call you." He sounded excited, but that was nothing unusual.

"I was consoling an unhappy real-estate wizard," I said. "What's up?"

"Just a little while ago, everyone came out of the house in a big hurry and took off in the Pontiac. I'm tailing them right now."

"Where are you?"

"Driving west on Fourth Avenue. I figure they're headed for the Government Bridge."

"Or they might keep going to the Centennial Bridge, just to keep us guessing. I'll stay on the phone."

"Okay." There was a period of silence. I started the engine, pulled away from the curb, and headed down Second Street.

"Mike."

"Yes."

"They're turning toward Arsenal Island. They're going to take the Government Bridge."

"Good. Stay with them and let me know which way they turn when they reach the other end and I'll pick them up on this side." A few minutes of silence passed.

"Mike."

"Yeah?"

"Trouble."

"How so?"

"The swingspan is opening. I'm losing them."

"That's the trouble with rivers. Too many boats. I'll catch them on this side." I wasn't far from the bridge. If I was lucky, I'd get there just as the Pontiac reached the Iowa side.

I wasn't lucky.

A red light and a dump truck spoiled my plan. By the time I got to the bridge, the Pontiac was nowhere in sight. I stopped on Second Street and waited for Carlos. Across the river, a towboat was pushing fifteen barges past the swingspan and into Lock 15. Finally, the span swung back around, and in a few minutes Carlos came off the bridge, parked his car, and joined me in the Chevy. "We lost them," I said.

"I guess so," he said.

"You know what I'm going to do?"

"No."

"I'm going home to bed and I suggest you do the same. We'll both function better after a little sleep. Tonight we can go after them again. Okay?"

"Okay, Mike."

I drove home, climbed into bed, and slept like a stump. I had retreated, temporarily abandoning the field to all the other stumps. If Max Brady wanted to load up the whole town and sell it to Nebraska, I wasn't going to do a thing about it for at least eight hours.

※

Night had fallen by the time I woke up. Saturday night. The lights on the bridges reflected off the river. I fixed myself a bowl of cereal, a stack of toast, a glass of orange juice, and a pot of coffee. There's nothing like the dinner hour to stimulate your appetite for breakfast.

I phoned Carlos, then showered, shaved, and got dressed. The night was waiting for me, with its usual collection of criminals, hustlers, and drug gangs. I walked down the two flights of stairs, stopping to say hello to Mr. Weaver, but declining his offer of bourbon and water. I never drink right after breakfast.

I walked out the front door and stopped on the sidewalk. My apartment building stands close to the street, the way apartment buildings are supposed to. No grass, geraniums, or trees. Just building, sidewalk, street. I was the only person outside. The sky was clear, the night quiet.

Down the street to the left, a car engine started. Headlights came on. The car pulled away from the curb and headed my way. Someone out for an evening drive or a night on the town. Fall is a wonderful time of year.

Suddenly, the car accelerated. The engine roared. I threw myself onto the sidewalk and rolled behind a Buick parked at the curb. The car flew past, a torrent of gunfire coming from the windows. I came up on one knee behind the Buick, discovered my automatic in my right hand, and emptied it into the back of the retreating car. I didn't know if I'd hit anyone, but the car would definitely need body work.

The Buick that had saved my life looked pretty sad, too, but I didn't have time to find the owner. I didn't think the thugs in the car would come by for another round of target practice, but I reloaded my automatic just in case. Then I trotted down the sidewalk to the Chevy. All along the street, people were peering out their windows. As I drove away, I heard the wail of a siren.

Chapter Twenty-Eight

I took the Memorial Bridge across the river and drove to the bungalow in East Moline. Carlos was already there, parked in the darkness beneath a huge oak tree. I stopped behind him, walked up, and slid into the front seat. Half a block in front of us, the bungalow was as dark as Point Barrow at midnight.

"Have you seen anyone?" I asked.

"No," Carlos said. "Nobody inside or out. No lights on. No car in the drive."

"They're probably out celebrating my death."

"Your what?" He turned toward me and stared, even though it was too dark to see much of anything inside the car.

"Somebody just tried to blow me away in front of my apartment."

"Who was it?"

"I don't know, but I'm betting that Max Brady sent someone to kill me after I insulted his girlfriend. She's George Mann's secretary, which means she told Brady exactly how much he could get for the dumps in the River Village Addition. That's why I'm betting Max was responsible for the gunfire."

"You want me to ask around?"

"Please do. This is too much fun for me."

"I don't know if anyone will be willing to talk."

"Don't be afraid to spend some money."

"Did you get hurt?"

"No, I'm okay, but somebody's Buick isn't. It got between me and some bullets."

"Did the police show up?"

"I'm sure they did, but I didn't wait around to answer their questions. I can't spare the time. Things are moving too fast."

"I guess so."

"Just for drill, let's take a closer look at the house."

We got out and went to all three doors, stopping to knock on each one. No one asked us in. I was tempted to kick in the back door, but the neighbors were all awake and bound to notice. We went back to Carlos's car and stood in the darkness.

"Stay here," I said. "They're not likely to come back anytime soon, but you never know. Call me if anything happens."

I climbed into the Chevy and drove back to Davenport, taking care to stay away from the shooting gallery in front of my apartment. The police would still be lurking about, full of questions and suspicions. Gunfire makes them nervous.

I drove up to Clay Street, parked the car, and got out. Brady's brick cottage was as dark and silent as the bungalow in East Moline. I walked around to the back door, which was hidden by the garage and a tall hedge. I didn't plan to leave without going through that door.

It was easier than I expected. The door was standing wide open. I couldn't see a light on anywhere inside. Slowly, cautiously, I crept through the door and waited for my eyes to adjust to the near-total darkness. Finally, I could make out enough shapes to move around. I walked from room to room until I reached a bedroom in the rear. The shades were drawn. No amount of waiting would ever allow me to see in that darkness. I switched on my pocket flashlight.

You never get used to it, no matter how many times you find one. You see live bodies all day long. They walk, sit, eat, talk—all the things you expect from them. The shock of finding another human being who will never do any of those things again is worse than anything else I know of. This one was lying on the bed, flat on his back, a butcher knife buried in his chest. Max Brady needed just one final piece of real estate—six feet deep.

Chapter Twenty-Nine

After finding Brady in his house on Clay Street, I flipped on the lights and examined the body. The knife, buried to the hilt, had the unmistakable wooden handle of the Gerhart-Brooks brand. I found no other wounds.

I looked around the room. No signs of a struggle. I looked in the drawers and closets, but found nothing useful. I looked under the bed and the rest of the furniture. Nothing at all.

After searching the bedroom, I walked around the rest of the house, turning on the lights and looking everywhere I could. In a desk drawer that I had searched during my previous visit, I found something new: numerous drugs of the kind you can't get without a prescription, plus several more of the kind you can't get even with a prescription.

I didn't find anything else, so I put everything back where I'd found it and called the police. The first squad car arrived in one minute. Keep that in mind the next time you need the police. Find a dead body and they'll come right over.

Lieutenant Rocco arrived twenty minutes later. His shirt could have used the touch of a hot iron. He walked into the bedroom and lit a cigarette. I didn't tell him we were in a smoke-free environment. "Mike," he said, "this is the third guy you've found with a knife in his chest. Knives like they sell at Morco Drugstores. I see a pattern developing."

"I see what you mean, Rocco. Repetition. Sameness."

"If I weren't married to your sister, I might wonder if you'd inserted those knives yourself. In fact, I'm starting to wonder in spite of your sister." He took a puff on the cigarette.

"Rocco," I said, "word of honor. I didn't do it."

"Then who did?" He scratched his chin.

"I used to suspect Brady, but that's no longer possible. It looks like a nut case. Someone with a list of victims all picked out."

"Who's next on the list?"

"I don't know, but I think I'll sleep on my stomach tonight."

Rocco grunted. "Something else, Mike. You don't know anything about the gunfire in front of your apartment building tonight, do you? The neighbors say it sounded like the Battle of Antietam."

"Sorry. I missed it."

"I'll bet. Where were you?"

"Looking for a chiropractor."

He motioned toward the corpse. "What does this have to do with the murders of Jason King and Joe Meiers?" he said.

"That's what I'm trying to find out," I said.

"Is Morrison involved in some way?"

"Don't know that either."

"Get out of here, Mike."

I got out.

⸙

I took Sunday off. The phone woke me at nine o'clock Monday morning. Morrison's secretary said the big guy wanted to see me right away.

I arrived at his office an hour later. For once he didn't keep me waiting. He spoke with his usual tone of self-importance. "Mike, this whole affair is starting to affect our business."

"It's starting to affect the mortuary business, too," I said.

"Your name has been mentioned in the news in connection with both Meiers and Brady, which automatically draws attention to Morco."

"What about Jason King's murder? You forgot to mention that. I didn't draw attention to Morco then. He was killed in a Morco store. A Gerhart-Brooks butcher knife drew all the attention needed. The only way to divert attention away from Morco is to find the killer. Then the press will focus on him and forget about us."

It was the word "us" that calmed him down. I saw it on his face. "Us" is a useful word. It creates a sense of shared interests and group resolve, whether they actually exist or not.

"How much longer will it take?" he said.

"We're getting close," I said. "People are getting nervous, starting to blow their cover. It won't take much longer." We talked awhile more. Then he let me go. I went down in the elevator and walked out into the sunlight. I hadn't been entirely frank with Morrison. With Max Brady now lying in the morgue, I had no idea who the killer was.

Chapter Thirty

The obituary in the *Quad-City Times* lacked some of the usual details. It didn't say where or when Brady was born. It didn't mention his parents or where he went to school. It said nothing about his mysterious career as a chiropractor. All it covered was his real-estate business in the Quad Cities, and it didn't say a hell of a lot about that. Conspicuously absent were any references to the Gentleman's Retreat and the Marquette Hotel, neither of which was a triumph of gracious living and community betterment. The obituary said nothing about Brady's survivors, if any.

One week after the killing, I sat in the Chevy, watching through my binoculars as six men carried Brady's casket to a fresh grave. It was early afternoon. Across the graveyard, tall narrow trees pointed at the blue sky. A clergyman stopped beside the grave, along with a small crowd: a few employees from the Gentleman's Retreat, desk clerk Fred Hutz from the Marquette Hotel, secretary Rita Vermilion, Jutjaw Kesler in his muscle suit, and a few people I didn't know. Standing near the clergyman, Kathy Dove-Linn and a woman with auburn hair consoled each other. I looked twice just to make sure. The woman with auburn hair was the redoubtable Carlotta Morrison.

My phone rang. "Can you see them, Mike?" Carlos said.

"Quite well," I said. "Some look sad. Some look thirsty. I think the thirsty outnumber the sad."

"I'll follow Kathy when she leaves."

"I thought you would."

The ceremony didn't last long. I assume the clergyman knew the futility of praying for Brady's soul, although he probably did it anyway. The crowd drifted away. Carlotta and Kathy left together, with Jutjaw driving and Carlos following. I had some questions for Carlotta, but they could wait. I knew how to find her. Rita Vermilion left with Fred Hutz. She needed a dry hankie. He needed a dry martini.

After everyone else had left, two middle-aged men in work clothes began lowering the casket into the grave. I got out of the car to look around. Graveyards help a person sort out his priorities. Annuities and mutual funds don't count for much in a graveyard. Life and death are the compelling themes.

Not far from Brady's grave, I came across the grave of Joe Meiers. Someone had paid for a small tombstone. I wondered who. As far as I knew, Meiers had no family and his friends had no money.

Not far away, I came to a newer grave, this one for Karl Deutsch. I felt a momentary ripple of fear, as if he might reach out of the grave and snap my spine.

The sensation of fear passed, and I walked closer. Deutsch had a larger tombstone than Meiers. The mound of earth hadn't settled much yet, and wilted flowers still covered it. Something else caught my eye, and I bent down to look. In the middle of the dead flowers, a small patch of bare earth was visible. Sticking out of the dirt was the distinctive handle of a Gerhart-Brooks butcher knife.

\

I went back to the office, looked up a number in the yellow pages, and dialed. "Gruber Monument Company," a female voice said.

"This is Thomas Meiers," I said. "I just learned of the death of my cousin Joseph Meiers, and I'd like to contribute to the cost of his gravestone."

"Just a moment, please, and I'll look up that account." There was a period of silence before she returned. "Mr. Meiers."

"Yes."

"Our records don't show a tombstone for a Joseph Meiers. How long ago did he die?"

"Just a few weeks ago."

"Then I'm afraid we didn't erect the monument. Sorry."

"That's all right. I must've written down the wrong company."

I looked up another number and dialed. There were only six monument companies in the Quad Cities, so it wouldn't take long. On the third try, I got lucky with the Peterson Monument Company.

"Yes, we have an account for Joseph Meiers," a woman said, "but the stone has already been paid for."

"Could you tell me who did it? I feel so guilty about this. I really want to contribute. I didn't even know Joe was dead until after his funeral."

"I understand. Let me look." She paused. "Here it is. The stone was paid for by Carlotta Morrison."

"Of course," I said. "Carlotta. The most thoughtful person in the family. Thank you very much."

I said goodbye, hung up, and leaned back in the chair. Good old Carlotta. The most thoughtful person in the family. I'd have to talk to Carlotta about her thoughtfulness for Joe Meiers, Kathy Dove, and anyone else I could think of.

I also wanted to find out who had paid for the stone for Karl Deutsch's grave, but I didn't think the ladies at the monument companies would believe my story twice in one day. So I sat tight and waited for Carlos to call. Two hours later, he finally did.

"Where are you?" I said.

"Outside the bungalow in East Moline," he said.

"What's going on?"

"Jutjaw drove Kathy and Carlotta to the Peterson Monument Company in Rock Island. Guess who met them there."

"Edgar Allan Poe."

"Rita Vermilion and Fred Hutz. They stayed about an hour. Then they all came over here and went inside. A little while later, Carlotta Morrison came out and drove away in her car."

"Alone?"

"Yes. I don't know where she went."

"That's okay. I can find her."

"Shall I stay here to see what develops?"

"Might as well, but tonight you need to get back on the street to see what the punks are saying. Now that Brady is dead, they might be talkative."

"Okay."

"Be careful."

I locked the office and drove up East River Drive. Carlotta's assistant was sweeping the floor when I arrived. She glanced up at me and went back to work without missing a stroke. Carlotta was at the rear of the store, examining a small fat pot. I walked back and kissed her on the lips. I knew it might be our last kiss, so I made it a good one. "Carlotta," I said, "we need to talk."

She led me into her office and sat down behind her desk. I closed the door and sat down across from her. Paintings by local artists hung on the walls—a river scene, a street scene, an impressionistic still life, an abstract something. The furniture was contemporary and expensive. "Well," she said, "your greeting was friendly, but your tone was formal. What do you want to talk about?"

"I saw you at Max Brady's funeral this afternoon. I couldn't help noticing the motherly way you looked after Kathy Dove or Linn or whatever her name is. I think you'd better tell me what's going on."

"What makes you think anything is going on? It isn't unusual to attend a funeral."

"Carlotta, three people have been stabbed to death in this town in the last few weeks, and at the cemetery today, I noticed that someone has stabbed the grave of the already-dead Karl Deutsch, someone apparently unhappy that he didn't get to kill him before the steroids did."

This got her attention, so I kept at it. "We're dealing with a madman here, and he apparently likes his work. If we don't find out who he is, he's going to keep killing people, and one of those people might be you or Kathy Dove or someone else too young and beautiful to die. You'd better tell me the truth about Kathy while you still can."

She looked at me for ten or fifteen seconds, apparently trying to decide something. Finally, she spoke. "I guess it doesn't matter anymore, now that they're all dead. But I don't want to see all this on the evening news."

"I'll keep it entirely to myself," I said, not really knowing if I could.

"Kathy Dove, as you've guessed, is my daughter, my only child. I got pregnant twenty years ago and left town to have the baby. The plan was to put the child up for adoption, but when the time came, I couldn't do it. I secretly brought her back here and made arrangements for her care."

"Now comes the hard part. Who was her father? Jason King?"

"That's what he thought." She smiled. "But he was wrong."

"Then who was it? Max Brady? Did you know him back then?"

"I knew him. We met in Chicago one summer. He thought he was her father, too, but he was mistaken." She smiled again. She was enjoying this. I wasn't.

"Is that why he moved here?"

"Yes, although he didn't move here immediately."

"So if he wasn't the father, who was? I need to know everything if I'm going to find the killer."

"Karl Deutsch."

"Karl Deutsch?" I sat there with my mouth open.

She laughed. "Men are always surprised when women take lovers who are attractive but stupid. But why shouldn't we? Men do it. They shack up with beautiful boneheads every time they get the chance."

"Did you buy Deutsch's tombstone?"

"Yes. Is there anything wrong with that?"

"Not a thing. Just wondered. What about Joe Meiers? You paid for his stone, too."

"What about him?"

"He wasn't attractive and stupid. In fact, he was quite a mess when I saw him."

"He wasn't always a mess."

"You're kidding."

She shook her head.

"You do get around, don't you?" I said.

"And don't you?" she said.

I hesitated. "I guess I do, don't I?" I felt my face turning red.

"Then don't act superior."

"Sorry. Let's stay on the topic. Did you know that Max Brady sometimes posed as a chiropractor?"

"I didn't know it, but it doesn't surprise me. He was very smart. He could fool anyone whenever he wanted."

"What about his connection with Doctor Barber at the Prairie Flower Chiropractic Clinic in Moline?"

"I don't know."

"You don't? Kathy goes there all the time. Does she have a bad back?"

"I don't think so." She seemed genuinely surprised.

"Who would have recommended Barber to her?"

"I have no idea."

"Max Brady?"

"I suppose he could have."

"Why did you let both King and Brady assume that Kathy was their daughter when you knew she wasn't?"

If this question embarrassed Carlotta, she didn't show it. "I wanted to make sure she was well cared for," she said. "Despite their flaws, both Jason and Max had a sense of responsibility. Karl knew he was really her father. That's why he looked after her so carefully. But he didn't have the money that King and Brady had, especially not when she was a little girl."

"Does she know who her real father was?"

"Yes."

"Her mother?"

"Yes."

"Why did all of you let her work in a strip joint?"

Carlotta looked down for a moment, then back at me. "She wanted to do it. We all tried to stop her, but she's very strong-willed. And a little crazy."

"How so?"

"For one thing, she's a kleptomaniac. Karl had to follow her around, paying off merchants to keep her out of jail and her name out of the news."

"And what exactly is her name?"

"Katherine Deutsch. That's the name I gave her when she was born in New York, but we always used the name Kathy Dove here, with occasional variations."

"Like Kathy Linn?"

She nodded. "That's right."

"Who pays off the merchants now that Deutsch is pumping steroids in paradise?"

"I do. Want to help?" She paused, but I didn't respond. "Now that you know, you'll feel responsible, too, won't you?"

"No, I won't. The last thing I need is another shoplifter to deal with. Actually, it sounds like a job for Carlos Lorca. He'd follow her through Hell if he had to, just in case she stole the matches."

"Sign him up." She smiled when she said this, although I think she really meant it.

"Was Kathy telling the truth when she said that Meiers paid her to distract me the night King was killed, or was that just an excuse for her shoplifting?"

"She was telling the truth. She told me all about it, and she's very worried." Carlotta looked worried herself as she told me this. "Meiers paid her a hundred dollars. She had no idea a murder would take place. She thought it was just a joke, an act you and she were putting on to fool Jason. Now she's afraid the police will think she was responsible for the murder."

"Why would Meiers cook up something like that?"

"He told her he was paid by someone else to make the arrangements, but he wouldn't say who."

"That's unfortunate."

"I guess it is."

"If she's telling the truth, the 'someone else' who paid Meiers is the person using all the butcher knives."

Chapter Thirty-One

It rained the next day from morning to night. I spent most of the day in the office, happy to stay dry. After lunch, I called Vic Domino. "Vic," I said, "what did you find out about the people on the list I gave you?"

"A very secretive group, Mike. People who use aliases. People who cover their tracks. But I still came up with a few things."

"Let's hear them."

"First of all, I got into the bank account for the Prairie Flower Chiropractic Clinic. Their deposits rose from fifty thousand dollars the first year of operation to three hundred thousand the second year, spaced out over all twelve months. Not bad for a new practice with only one doctor."

"Not bad for a place where the waiting room is always empty. Sounds like a laundry to me."

"I also got into one of Brady's accounts. His businesses are very lucrative, too, especially the Gentleman's Retreat and the Marquette Hotel. Hundreds of thousands every year."

"More laundry work," I said.

"No doubt," he said.

"Good going, Vic. What else do you have?"

"Rebecca King has a long psychiatric record. So does Kathy Dove."

"Diagnoses?"

"Don't know. All I have is records of insurance payments."

"Go on."

"Joe Meiers used to be a chiropractor."

"You're kidding."

"Nope. Very successful for several years. Then he declared bankruptcy. I don't know why."

"Probably drank all the profits. What else, Vic?"

"Fred Hutz has a prison record."

"What for?"

"Mail fraud, one of your more genteel criminal activities."

"Very tasteful. Anything else?"

"I discovered one interesting fact while checking educational records. Several people on your list went to high school together at Davenport West."

"Who are they?"

"Jason King, Rebecca King, Karl Deutsch, Joe Meiers, Fred Hutz, Brian Walker, Tracy Gibbs, Carlotta Morrison, and George Mann, although Mann dropped out in his senior year. You went to Davenport Central, by the way, just in case you forgot."

"Thanks, Vic. What was my grade-point average?"

"Three-point-one. Not so hot in an age of inflated grading."

"Too many girlfriends. They wouldn't leave me alone. Anything else?"

"That's it so far. You want me to keep looking? I can't promise much more."

"Yeah, stay at it awhile longer. And try not to find my bar bill at the Blackhawk Hotel."

An hour later, Carlos appeared at the door, armed with a wet umbrella. He was grinning like a kid in an icecream factory, so I knew he had something good to tell me. He sat down on the other side of the desk. "Hello, Mike," he said.

"Hello, Carlos," I said. "What's up?"

"I spent the night in Rock Island."

"Sorry to hear it. You have my sympathy."

"I got something on Brady. You were right. Now that's he's dead, the punks are willing to talk, for a price."

"Of course."

"The word is that he was bringing drugs in from Chicago for sale in the Quad Cities. It was a big operation, and we can expect more dead bodies before someone else takes over." Carlos grinned again. He'd earned his pay this time.

"What did he do with the cash?" I said.

"They say he laundered it through his various businesses." Carlos smoothed his tie, the one with the soccer balls. "And, it appears, through the Prairie Flower Chiropractic Clinic."

"And I know who delivered the cash."

"Who?"

"Sorry, Carlos. I suspect Kathy Dove."

"No."

"I'm afraid so." Carlos looked sad. "Why else would someone in perfect health visit a doctor so often, especially someone associated with Max Brady?"

"She probably didn't know what the money was from."

"Maybe not." I didn't know what Kathy knew and what she didn't, but I was happy to agree with Carlos if it made him feel better. "What else did you find?"

"Brady hired the punks who tried to gun you down the other night after your run-in with Rita Vermilion. You were getting too close to the truth for his liking, and he was afraid you'd go to the police."

"Anything about his succession of chiropractic offices?"

Carlos looked at me as if I had completely missed the point. "No, Mike. No one said anything about that."

"Just curious. Did anyone know where he was from?"

"As a matter of fact, one kid saw a postcard on the dashboard of Brady's car one day. It was from his mom in Tipp City, Ohio. The kid wrote down the return address in case he ever wanted to blackmail Brady."

"Very resourceful, but now he won't get the chance."

"I know."

"How much did you pay him for the address?"

"Four hundred."

"That should make up for part of his lost opportunity. Was he satisfied?"

"He didn't complain."

I flew to Dayton, Ohio, on Saturday. Clouds and planes were sailing east in a blue sky. The drive from the airport to Tipp City took about five minutes. I pulled off the freeway shortly after two in the afternoon and drove down the main street of the little town, from the ugly shopping center at one end to the old mill at the other. Tipp City was quiet that day. I got the impression it was always quiet. Twenty years before I would have seen that as a problem. Now I saw it as a blessing.

I drove to the block where Brady's mother lived on the south side of town. At first I had trouble finding the right address, but a little dark-eyed girl named Gina helped me. I walked up the sidewalk to the small white house, which looked newly painted. The porch showed signs of recent repairs by a good carpenter.

The postcard Carlos had told me about didn't have the sender's name on it. It was signed only "Mom." The name on the mailbox beside the door was "Baldwin." I knocked, and a woman about seventy years old came to the door. "Yes?" she said.

"Hello, Mrs. Baldwin," I said. "My name is Michael Scofield. I'm a private investigator from Davenport, Iowa. I have some bad news for you about your son."

"You mean David?" She looked shocked already. She knew what the bad news would be. People always do.

"He called himself Max Brady in Davenport. I didn't know his real name."

"Yes, that's the name he told me to use when I wrote to him. What happened to him?"

"I'm afraid he's dead. He asked me to contact you if this ever happened."

She began to cry. I stepped inside and helped her over to the couch. I'd planned ahead, bringing along a package of kleenex in my jacket pocket. I gave her a couple and sat down on the couch to wait out the storm. The couch was nice, but too big for the small room. A large-screen TV stood along the opposite wall.

Finally, she blew her nose and looked at me. "How did he die?"

"He was murdered, stabbed to death." This summoned more tears. I handed her another kleenex and waited awhile longer.

She blew her nose again. "I'm really not surprised," she said. "Sad but not surprised. He started hanging out with a bad crowd a long time ago, right after he dropped out of school."

"Where was that?" I said.

"The Hilton College of Chiropractic in Cincinnati. He did real well at first. We were so proud of him. But he got into trouble his second year. They accused him of cheating. Then they said he stole some equipment and sold it. None of it was true, of course, but they said it was. He wanted to succeed so much. I guess he did later. He's been sending me money for years. His father died, you know, not long after David moved to Chicago."

"What did he do in Chicago?"

"He never told me. I asked him several times, but he wouldn't say."

"Do you have any idea who might have wanted to kill him?"

"No. All I know is that he desperately wanted to be a chiropractor. He read a book by B.J. Palmer when he was in high school, and that's what got him started. When he went away to school in Cincinnati, he told me all about it. He talked about the spine and subluxations and all kinds of things I couldn't understand. He lost his enthusiasm for life when they kicked him out. I could tell."

"Did he ever talk about it after that?"

"Only once. Not long ago, he said he loaned money to a young man who was starting a practice in the Quad Cities. He seemed proud of that, that he could help someone who was just starting out."

"Very kind of him," I said. "Did he say who the man was?"

"No, he didn't say." She started to cry again and I handed her another kleenex. "All he ever wanted to do was become a chiropractor," she said. "Somehow that doesn't seem like too much to ask."

Chapter Thirty-Two

I thought about David Baldwin as the plane carried me toward O'Hare the next morning. By now it was obvious why he had chosen the name "Brady" as his last alias. Brady Street is a main thoroughfare in Davenport. It's also the street on which the Palmer College of Chiropractic is located. Given what Mrs. Baldwin had told me, this name would have held special meaning for her son, the boy who, because of some strange obsession, wanted more than anything to become a chiropractor.

I arrived at the Quad City Airport shortly before noon. The day was cool and cloudy. I called Carlos and told him to meet me at the office the next morning. Then I called Carlotta.

ℷ

At ten-thirty Monday morning, I climbed the stairs from Fourth Street and walked down the hallway to the office. I was unlocking the door when the floor creaked behind me. I turned, expecting to see Carlos, and saw instead the face of Bobby Jutjaw Kesler. But I didn't see his left fist. It was moving too fast. It hit me in the right temple and was quickly followed by his right fist, which hit me in the other temple. I was headed for the floor when his foot caught me squarely in the belly.

As I gasped for breath, I heard something solid hitting what sounded like a human skull. I assumed the skull was my own until Jutjaw fell to the floor beside me and went to sleep. Standing over him was the best detective I'd ever seen—little Carlos Lorca with a big, strong club.

"Carlos," I said as I tried to sit up, "where did you get that wonderful club?"

"It's part of the handrail from the stairway. We'll have to fix it."

"Don't worry about it. I'd much rather fall down the stairs than have Jutjaw kick me in the stomach."

I sat there until the floor stopped moving. Carlos called the police, and when they arrived we told them exactly what had happened. Just for color, I added the fact that Jutjaw had been closely associated with Max Brady and might know something about his drug business. For background information, I suggested they call Police Chief Walter Metcalf in Savanna, Illinois, and ask about Bobby Kesler.

The cops hauled Jutjaw away, and Carlos took me to the emergency room at St. Luke's, where we had two hours of jokes and x-rays. Then we drove to the Prairie Flower Chiropractic Clinic in Moline.

\

Ms. Barber stood up and stared when she saw me. "You look awful," she said. "What happened?"

"I ran into a gorilla," I said. "It happens much too often."

"You should see a doctor." She looked at Carlos, then back at me.

"I already did. I'll live about twenty minutes, just long enough to talk to your husband about Max Brady."

"He's with a patient."

"I bet he is. I'll give him two minutes. Then I'm going in like the Green Bay Packers. Tell him to pop some vertebrae and get ready."

She went away, came back a minute later, and told us to follow her.

Dr. Barber was waiting at the door of his office. We went inside and closed the door. The doctor and I sat down. Carlos remained standing in order to catch me if I fell off the chair.

"What's this all about?" Dr. Barber said. "I don't like people bursting in on me like this."

"What it's all about is the late Max Brady, also known as James White, Peter O'Brien, et cetera, and known by his mother as David Baldwin. I didn't see you at his funeral the other day. Rather thoughtless of you, wasn't it?"

"Why should I attend his funeral? I didn't even know him."

"If you didn't know him, why did he give you two hundred and fifty thousand dollars? You don't give that kind of money to someone you don't know." He started to protest, but I cut him off. "Don't deny it. It's all there in the bank records." I wasn't entirely sure what was in the bank records, but I thought it was worth a bluff. The bluff worked.

"Someone loaned me the money to keep the office going. Business hasn't been all that great. There's too much competition in the Quad Cities."

"Was it a loan, or was it just another way for Brady to launder the piles of money his punks collected on the streets? You probably figure now that he's dead you can just keep it all for yourself and never pay it back. And maybe you can, unless we decide to tell the police where you got it. That's drug money, you know. The feds can seize the whole amount, plus every gadget and every stick of furniture in this place."

Most people aren't very good actors, and Dr. Barber was no exception. As soon as I mentioned the feds taking his gadgets, his face fell a foot and a half. "I don't know what you're talking about," he finally said, trying to regain his professional demeanor.

"Don't lie to me!" I shouted. "Some lunatic is sticking people full of holes, and I have to find out who. Anyone could be next. You. Your wife. Anyone. Tell me about Brady or kiss your tidy little office goodbye."

"Brady lent me the money. It was his idea. He said he just wanted to help. That's all there was to it."

"That's all there was to it? He just walked in one day and said, 'Hi, I'm Max Brady. How would you like to have two hundred and fifty thousand dollars in small bills?' Do you really expect anyone to believe that?"

"No, it wasn't like that. Talk to Rita Vermilion. She was Brady's girlfriend. She's the one who first suggested it. My wife was talking to her one day about how expensive everything was, and Rita said she knew somebody who might be willing to help. That's exactly how it happened. I swear to God. And that's all I know."

"Didn't you think it strange that Kathy Dove delivered this loan, in cash, over the course of an entire year? Is that the way loans are usually handled?"

"I was desperate. I didn't ask questions."

"I don't believe you. I think we should invite your wife in to discuss this. Carlos, would you—"

"No, wait!" Barber said. He rubbed his forehead and sighed. "She doesn't know the truth about this. She really did talk to Rita. She thinks Brady is just lending us the money."

"Even though Kathy Dove gave it to you in cash?"

"Kathy never gave the money to my wife. She always scheduled an appointment and gave the money directly to me."

"How much did Brady pay you?"

"Ten percent of the amount deposited. There was a lot of money, so it added up. It's what kept us from going broke."

"I'm sure it did, but that doesn't make it right."

He looked away. "I know." I stood up, and he looked back at me. "What are you going to do?" he said. I didn't answer. "Are you going to tell my wife?"

"No, not now anyway."

"Are you going to tell the police?"

"I don't know." Carlos and I headed for the door. My head felt like a bad day in hell and my stomach felt worse, but I had to see Rita Vermilion.

We knew Jutjaw wouldn't be there to break our legs and twist our heads off, so Carlos and I walked right up to the bungalow in East Moline.

I knocked on the front door, but no one answered. We went around to the back. The door was open, but the screen door was closed and locked. I knocked. No one came. I knocked again. Still no one. Time for direct action. I kicked a hole in the screen, reached in, unlocked the door, and walked in with Carlos right behind me.

We walked through the house to the darkened living room, where someone was watching a soap opera on TV. She sat in an easy chair with her back to us, curly black hair tumbling down her beautiful neck. "Hello, Rita," I said.

She jumped up and spun around. "Oh, it's you," she said.

"Please," I said, "a little more warmth if you don't mind. Carlos and I might get the idea you don't like us, and that could damage our self-esteem. And as a soap-opera viewer, you must know how critical that is to our social development."

"Screw your social development."

"Okay. Let's talk about your upcoming prison sentence. Mind if I sit down?" She didn't answer. I sat down anyway, in a rocking chair facing her, and she sat back down in the easy chair. Carlos stayed on his feet, staring at Rita. He was probably comparing her with Kathy Dove, ranking them both on a scale of one to infinity. My head hurt too much for arithmetic. "Carlos," I said, "could you

turn off the idiot box before we all get brain damage." He switched
it off.

I stared through the dimness at Rita. "I'm sorry about Max," I
said. "I know you were fond of him."

"Go screw yourself."

I ignored this suggestion. "You may not know it, but you're
in deep trouble. As Brady's girlfriend, you were privy to his drug
dealing, disaster fraud, and real-estate schemes. Not to mention
impersonating a chiropractor. When I tell the authorities about
all this, they're going to come after you with dogs and tanks. So
let's not play games here. Three people have been stabbed to death
in the last few weeks, and I feel compelled to find out who did it."

She looked as if she almost believed me. "I'm absolutely serious,"
I said. "I'll turn you over to the cops right now if I have to. I'll do
anything it takes. I'll make it up as I go along, invent evidence as
the need arises. I'm good at that, Rita. And you know what? The
cops will believe me. You mean nothing to me. I don't care what
happens to you. Why shouldn't I turn you in?"

She stared at me. I had on my tough-guy look. She looked at
Carlos. He nodded. "All right," she said.

"What do you know about Karl Deutsch, Joe Meiers, and
Jason King?"

"I don't know anything about Deutsch, except that he drove
Kathy Dove around town. Joe Meiers was a drunk. He did odd
jobs for Max when he was sober enough. He was an old friend of
Jason King's. I saw them together a few times. I think King loaned
him money."

"None of this is very exciting, Rita. I need information about rivalries, hatreds, double-dealings—the kind of stuff that makes people kill each other."

"There's one other thing."

"Yes?"

"Jason found out that Brady was taking advantage of Morrison in the sale of all those houses in the River Village Addition. Joe Meiers probably told him. Brady paid King a pile of money to keep him quiet. I know because Bobby Kesler and I took it to him."

"Did King know who was stealing drugs from the store?"

"I don't know."

"Did Brady pay him to keep quiet about that, too?"

She hesitated. "I'm not sure," she said. "Sorry."

"That's all right, Rita. I understand. It isn't healthy to know too much about illegal drugs." A fly circled my head and landed on my ear. I shooed it away. "Anything else you want to tell me?"

"No." She paused. "Are you satisfied?"

"Not entirely."

"Is there something else I should do?"

"Yes." The fly circled my head again.

"What?"

I stood up and brushed the fly away. "Get your screen door fixed."

†

We walked out to Carlos's car and climbed in. "Carlos," I said, "this case has more angles than a trigonometry book." As we were about to drive away, a strange car pulled up in front of the bungalow. Kathy Dove got out on the passenger's side. Then Tracy Gibbs, the cashier from the downtown Morco, climbed out on the driver's side. Finally, pharmacist Brian Walker climbed out of the back seat. They walked up to the house like old friends, two drug thieves and their compliant runner.

"You want to talk to them, Mike?" Carlos said.

"Waste of time," I said. "More lies from those three would only confuse us. Let's get out of here." There was someone else I wanted to see, but I decided to wait until the next day. My head felt like a sailor's after two-day leave.

Carlos drove me back across the Mississippi and stopped at the door to my apartment building. The front wall was scarred with bullet holes. My presence in the neighborhood had done nothing to raise property values. "Carlos," I said, "keep your eye on Rita Vermilion. I don't think she's telling us everything."

"Sure thing, Mike."

I looked around for teenagers with guns. The coast was clear, so I got out of the car and went inside. Mr. Weaver stopped me as I headed for the stairs. "Mike," he said, "you look like hell. You've got to take better care of yourself."

"You're absolutely right."

He gave me three shots of the best apricot brandy ever made and sent me up to bed.

Chapter Thirty-Three

It was only eleven o'clock on Tuesday morning, but Rebecca King was already drunk—stupid, sappy, slobbery drunk. She steered me over to the couch, sat down right beside me, and shoved a gin and tonic into my hand. Under the circumstances, there was nothing to do but drink it.

"You're kind of cute for a policeman," she said.

"I'm not really a policeman," I said. "I'm a private detective."

"Like Humphrey Bogart."

"Sort of, but without the sneer. I never do it right."

"What did you come to see me about, Bogey? Still looking for the bad guy, or are you looking for Becky?"

"Becky?" I took a drink.

"Me, silly, Rebecca."

"Oh, yes, of course, Becky." I took another drink. A big one this time.

"That's nice. You came to see Becky." She put her hand on my cheek and kissed me on the lips. It was a long, sour kiss. I was close to suffocation when she finally pulled back. I drained the glass and held it in front of her face before she could make another attack.

"You want another drink, Bogey? Let Becky get it for you." She stood up, took the glass, and walked away.

I sat up and looked around for some form of defense—a shield, a bookcase, a stone wall—anything. Nothing presented itself. Becky returned almost instantly. "Here you go," she said as she handed me the drink and sat down on my lap. She had put her own drink on the coffee table, leaving both hands free for the assault.

"Look, Becky," I said, talking through my glass, which I was again using defensively, "before we go on, there are some questions I need to ask you."

"Questions? Sure, Bogey. Shoot."

Becky's ample body held me like a boulder. I'd have to talk my way out of this one. "Becky," I said, taking a quick drink, "you told me you didn't think Jason was stealing drugs from the downtown store. If he wasn't, who was?"

"I don't know. Brian Walker, maybe. He always has a lot of gambling debts. Jason told me that a long time ago." She started to lean toward me, but I fended her off with the glass.

"Rita Vermilion says that Jason found out about one of Brady's questionable real-estate deals and Brady paid him off to keep him quiet. Do you think Jason would have accepted a bribe like that?"

"Probably, if there was no danger of getting caught."

"Do you know anything about it?"

"No." She planted another wet one on my mouth. After a lifetime she disengaged, and I took a drink.

"Are you sure you don't know anything?" I said.

"When did this happen?" she said.

"Within the last year."

"Then I'm sure. I hadn't talked to him recently. I like you better than him anyway."

She took aim at my mouth again, but I raised the glass and took a slurp. "What about Joe Meiers?"

"I like you better than him, too."

"No, I mean what do you know about him? Rita says he was an old friend of Jason's."

"I don't know anything about him, except that he went to the same high school I did. He was good looking back then. Before he became a drunk." She picked up her glass, took a drink, and put it back down. "Right after high school, he had an affair with Carlotta Morrison, the whore."

"Rita says Jason sometimes gave him money."

"Oh yeah? Who is this Rita?"

"She used to be George Mann's secretary. I'm sure he fired her by now, though."

"You don't like her better than me, do you?"

"Of course not, Becky."

"George Mann. What's old George up to these days?"

"Property management: fixing the gutters, taking out the trash. That sort of thing."

"I haven't seen boring old George for years. Does he still have a crush on Carlotta?"

"He didn't say. Should I ask him?" I drained the glass.

"Sure, Bogey, but not right now." She put my glass on the coffee table, pushed me down on the couch, and fell on top of me.

An hour later, I negotiated my release. Before letting me go, Becky made me promise to come back soon. I promised and I meant it, provided you think of "soon" in the geologic sense, as in "Soon the inland seas receded" or "Soon the Colorado River had carved out the Grand Canyon."

I drove downtown through a steady rain. The phone was ringing when I got to the office. "Mike," Carlos said, "guess what two people I just saw together?"

"Bud Abbott and Lou Costello. You shouldn't be watching old movies on the job, Carlos. It takes your mind off the toothpaste."

"Nope. Rita Vermilion and George Mann."

"Is that right?"

"Yes. He took her to coffee this morning. They were laughing and talking like old friends."

"That's strange. I thought he'd still be mad about her collusion with Brady."

"Not today, he wasn't."

"He must have forgiven her."

"That's how it looked," Carlos said.

I thought about this for a moment. "Unless *he* was conspiring with Brady, too," I said. "That's an angle I hadn't considered."

"Nothing would surprise me at this point, Mike."

"Me neither. Good work, Carlos. Stay with her."

I hung up the phone and began to pace, stopping occasionally to stare at the vacant building across the street. The people in this case were acting very strange, and I had to figure out why before someone else ended up with a knife in the chest. I was staring at the vacant building when an idea hit me. I grabbed the phone and dialed.

"Mr. Morrison's office," a woman's voice said.

"Barbara," I said, speaking quickly, "this is Mike Scofield. Let me talk to Morrison."

"I'm sorry, Mike, but he left about ten minutes ago."

"Did he say where he was going?"

"He said he had to meet someone at the River Village Addition."

The River Village Addition. Of course. Now it dawned on me who had left that Gerhart-Brooks butcher knife in the kitchen at 129 Rose Street, someone with easy access to that house.

I thanked Barbara and hung up. Then I tried to call Carlos, but he didn't answer. "God help us," I said. I ran down to the car and headed west on Second Street. Between Main and Harrison, a delivery truck blocked the way. I finally got around it, then had to wait for the stoplight at Harrison.

After negotiating the rest of the lights on Second Street, I finally turned down Rockingham Road. It had been raining all day, and now it began to pour. The windshield wipers slapped back and forth.

I fought my way through the traffic on Rockingham Road until I reached Rose Street, where I turned left and drove to the block at the far end. Morrison's eight square blocks of the River Village Addition looked different from the last time I'd seen them. Most of the houses had already been demolished. A bulldozer stood silently in the rain.

I spotted Morrison's car parked in front of the house at 129 Rose, one of the few houses left. Another car stood behind Morrison's. I had never seen it before, but I knew whose it was. I stopped the Chevy at the curb, took out my automatic, and ran through the rain to the house.

The front door was boarded up, so I ran around to the back, climbed the steps, and peeked through the open door. William Morrison and George Mann were talking and drinking coffee from styrofoam cups. Morrison said something and laughed at his own joke. Mann laughed, too, while resting his hand on one of the shelves.

Morrison took another drink of coffee and Mann moved toward him. I stepped through the doorway and saw the gleam of the butcher knife in his hand, ready to thrust. "Stop!" I shouted. He didn't do it. There was no time for another warning. I aimed and fired.

The slug hit Mann in the shoulder. By now Morrison had seen the knife and backed away. Mann stopped, turned, and came at me with all the force of a man cheated out of his life's goal. I held the automatic with both hands, aimed at his chest, and squeezed the trigger three times.

Mann slumped against the refrigerator, dropped the knife, and slid down to the floor. A red stain covered his chest. His eyes looked up at me. "Goddamn you," he said.

Then he died.

Chapter Thirty-Four

It was still raining. Rocco and I stood on the front porch of Mann's big Queen Anne house while his troops searched all three floors. "Rocco," I said, "it's really quite simple. What did all three victims have in common? They all had affairs with Carlotta Morrison. If you add Karl Deutsch, stabbed symbolically after burial, that makes four victims, all of whom had affairs with Carlotta. There was at least one more that I know of, but he got away alive."

"Who?" Rocco took a puff on his cigarette.

"I'm not at liberty to say."

A newspaper photographer pulled up in front and began taking pictures of the house. I turned my back to him. If you want Scofield's photo, you have to see his agent.

"But in all these romances," I said, "the one always left out was George Mann. Rebecca King told me he had had a crush on Carlotta. In fact, he dropped out of high school his senior year, and I'm guessing it was because Carlotta rejected him. His infatuation then apparently developed into a pathological obsession."

"Over the years," I said, "he began plotting the murder of every man who ever stood between him and Carlotta, ending with the worst offender of all, William Morrison himself. As a nice sick irony, he always used a knife from a Morco drugstore. He even committed the first murder in one of those stores, and he planned to kill Morrison in a house Morrison had recently purchased. Clever of him, huh?"

Rocco grunted and scratched his cheek.

"I realize some of this is speculation," I said, "but whatever his motives, there's no doubt that Mann was about to kill Morrison."

"Did Brady have anything to do with the deaths of King and Meiers?" Rocco said.

"I don't think so. Brady hired drive-by punks to try to kill me. Mann did his own work. With King and Meiers, he had additional motivation, not that he needed it."

"How so?"

"King found out about the flood-relief scam. Mann killed him, and Meiers knew it because he'd been involved in hiring Kathy Dove to distract me, although I'm sure he didn't know what Mann was planning to do. Mann had told him it was a 'joke.'" So both King and Meiers knew too much about Mann. But he would have killed them both anyway. His infatuation with Carlotta was the real motive."

After taking a final puff, Rocco flicked his cigarette into a puddle of rainwater on the lawn. "What about Brady's murder?" he said.

"The same was true with him. Brady and Mann conspired to milk Morrison for every dime they could get for the River Village properties, but that had nothing to do with why Mann killed Brady. He killed him for the same reason he killed the others.

"My problem," I said, "was that I always focused on Brady's involvement in the case and didn't notice Mann's. Brady would try anything—drug dealing, flood-relief fraud, real-estate scams. He even had goofy little Kathy Dove picking up stolen drugs from Tracy Gibbs and Brian Walker at the downtown Morco. Brady was guilty of so much that I assumed he was responsible for the murders."

I gave Kathy Dove's name to Rocco. I wasn't worried about what would happen to her. Her psychiatrist would keep her out of jail. But I didn't mention Dr. Barber. I know I should have, but I couldn't bear the thought of what it would do to his wife, and I figured he had learned his lesson. The police would probably nail him anyway, but if they did, it wouldn't be my responsibility. I can't solve all the world's problems. Ninety percent is as much as I can handle.

A detective sergeant stepped out onto the porch. "Lieutenant," he said, "I have something to show you."

"Wait here," Rocco said to me. I wasn't allowed in the house. I might knock down a wall or set the place on fire. Another photographer arrived, and I held a newspaper in front of my face.

In a few minutes, Rocco returned with the detective sergeant, who was carrying an ornate wooden box. "Mike," Rocco said, "take a look at this."

I walked over, and the detective opened the lid of the box. Inside was a piece of paper with a handwritten list of six names: Jason King, Joe Meiers, Karl Deutsch, Max Brady, William Morrison, and last of all, Mike Scofield. In addition to the list, the box contained one other object—Mann's last Gerhart-Brooks butcher knife.

⑂

The publicity that resulted from Mann's death was finally too much for Morrison. He divorced Carlotta. But he didn't fire me. I had saved his life, and he didn't want to appear ungrateful.

Despite my modesty around newspaper photographers, news of the case improved the fortunes of the Scofield Detective Agency, sending a number of new clients my way. As a result, I gave Carlos a raise and hired someone to clean the office once a week. The place now looks almost respectable. The phone rings every day, and sometimes we answer it.

Carlotta still has her gallery. When she gets bored, she puts on some dark-red lipstick, a pair of high heels, and a straight black skirt. In this disguise, she comes to the office and poses as my secretary—a film-noir vision from what must have been a better time than this.

Carlos still likes his job. He finally got up the nerve to ask Kathy Dove out on a date. They had dinner at the Blackhawk Hotel. Kathy stole the silverware, but Carlos returned it later.

Someday maybe I'll hire a full-time secretary and another detective and move into a bigger office, but for now everything seems to have fallen into place. People shoplift. Floods rise and fall. Carlotta gets more beautiful every day. And down in the River Village Addition, William Morrison is building the biggest shopping center in the West End.

The End

 **Patrick Irelan** began writing mysteries with a series of short stories. With two exceptions, each of these appeared in either *Ellery Queen's Mystery Magazine* or *Alfred Hitchcock's Mystery Magazine*. *The Big Drugstore* is his first mystery novel. He is also the author of two books of comic short stories— *Reruns* and *The Miracle Boy*. His two books of family memoir include *Central Standard* and *A Firefly in the Night*.

Detective Mike Scofield never rests,

Coming soon

Murder On Cork Hill

I was trying to organize some files when I heard the sound of footsteps coming down the hall. They were loud, like the sound made by high heels. I closed a drawer in my file cabinet and looked at the door, ready for the joy of money.

She opened the door and walked in without knocking. "Mr. Scofield?" she said.

"That's me," I said. Her appearance surpassed that of your average citizen. She could have been a movie star back in the middle of the Twentieth Century, someone like Jane Russell. A perfect nose, eyes more black than brown, and dark hair that fell to her shoulders in a graceful wave. Her features weren't delicate. They were more attractive than that. She was wearing a pale-blue spring dress that was far more conservative than Ms. Russell's famous attire in *The Outlaw*. I guessed her age at twenty-five.

I glanced down at her legs. From the altitude a pair of white pumps gave her, the calves of those legs had assumed a shapeliness that made me forget about Jane Russell. "Please have a seat," I said.

She sat down and crossed her legs. I tried not to stare. "I'm Angela Kelly," she said. "I need your help."

"Tell me about it."

The Ice Cube Press began publishing in 1993 to focus on how to live with the natural world and to better understand how people can best live together in the communities they share and inhabit. Using the literary arts to explore life and experiences in the heartland of the United States we have been recognized by a number of well-known writers including: Gary Snyder, Gene Logsdon, Wes Jackson, Patricia Hampl, Greg Brown, Jim Harrison, Annie Dillard, Ken Burns, Roz Chast, Jane Hamilton, Daniel Menaker, Kathleen Norris, Janisse Ray, Craig Lesley, Alison Deming, Harriet Lerner, Richard Rhodes, Michael Pollan, David Abram, David Orr, and Barry Lopez. We've published a number of well-known authors including: Mary Swander, Jim Heynen, Mary Pipher, Bill Holm, Connie Mutel, John T. Price, Carol Bly, Marvin Bell, Debra Marquart, Ted Kooser, Stephanie Mills, Bill McKibben, Craig Lesley, Elizabeth McCracken, Dean Bakopoulos, and Paul Gruchow. Check out Ice Cube Press books on our web site, join our facebook group, follow us on twitter, visit booksellers, museum shops, or any place you can find good books and discover why we continue striving to, "hear the other side."

Ice Cube Press, LLC (est. 1993)
205 N. Front Street
North Liberty, Iowa 52317-9302
steve@icecubepress.com
twitter @icecubepress
www.icecubepress.com

to Laura Lee & Fenna Marie
two investigative
clue searching miracles

OX (05/16)